Meteor Crater Museum,
Thursday, May 10, 2001

Meteor Crater Museum,
Thursday, May 10, 2001

Is There Life on Mars?

Is There

Life on Mars?

Dennis Brindell Fradin

Illustrated with full-color and black-and-white prints and photographs

Margaret K. McElderry Books

Margaret K. McElderry Books
An imprint of Simon & Schuster Children's Publishing Division
1230 Avenue of the Americas
New York, New York 10020
Copyright © 1999 by Dennis Brindell Fradin
Book design by Angela Carlino
The text of this book was set in Apollo
Printed in the United States of America
10 9 8 7 6 5 4 3 2 1
Library of Congress Cataloging-in-Publication Data
Fradin, Dennis B.
Is There Life on Mars? / Dennis Brindell Fradin ; illustrated
with full-color and black-and-white prints and photographs.
p. cm.
Includes bibliographical references and index.
Summary: Examines the theories about life on Mars, providing
both historical and current information about our exploration
of the Red Planet.
ISBN 0-689-82048-8
1. Mars (Planet)—Exploration—Juvenile literature. 2. Life on
other planets—Juvenile literature. [1. Mars (Planet)—
Exploration. 2. Space flight to Mars. 3. Life on other planets.]
I. Title.
QB641.F68   1999   919.9'2304—dc21   98-38208

FIRST
EDITION

For my lovely daughter, Diana Judith Fradin

Consultant: Dr. John Stansberry, Astronomer, Lowell Observatory

Acknowledgments
Research and photo acquisition: Judith Bloom Fradin

The author thanks his daughter, Diana Judith Fradin, for translating Camille Flammarion's books from the French.

The author also thanks:
Antoinette Beiser, Librarian, Lowell Observatory
Dr. Lisa R. Gaddis, Geologist, Astrogeology
    Program, United States Geological Survey
Martin D. Hecht, Archivist, Lowell Observatory
Stephanie Meyer of White Bear Lake, Minnesota
    (my twelve-year-old pen pal)
Dr. Susan Sakimoto, Universities Space
    Research Association at NASA's Goddard
    Space Flight Center in Greenbelt, Maryland
Dr. Gerald Soffen, Astrobiologist, NASA
Dr. John Spencer, Astronomer, Lowell
    Observatory
Dr. John Stansberry, Astronomer, Lowell
    Observatory
The children and faculty of West School in
    Glencoe, Illinois

Contents

introduction

Fascinating Red Planet

♂ **Since ancient times,** people have been fascinated by a reddish object in the night sky. Many stars are of similar color, but this heavenly body does not twinkle as stars do. The object that has long inspired awe is the Red Planet, Mars.

For centuries, Mars was the focus of our hopes and fears about extraterrestrials (beings from beyond Earth). Hopes, because we seem to have a deep-seated desire to find company in the Universe. Fears, because of the possibility that the Martians could conquer us.

The belief in the existence of Martians gained momentum in 1877, when the Italian astronomer Giovanni Schiaparelli observed a weblike network of lines crisscrossing Mars. The American astronomer Percival Lowell popularized the idea that the lines were canals built by intelligent beings to transport water across their dry planet. Lowell claimed the Martians were superior to Earthlings scientifically as well as physically, estimating that they stood nearly 20 feet tall and possessed the strength of fifty Earthmen.

Fantastic schemes were hatched to contact our planetary neighbors. One idea was to flash reflected sunlight at the Martians with giant mirrors. Another was to grow forests and wheat fields in huge geometric shapes that would be visible through Martian telescopes. Several scientists claimed to have detected messages *from* the Red Planet. When a shape resembling a *W* appeared on Mars in 1904, some people feared that it stood for *war* and that the Martians would soon attack Earth. People became so convinced of the existence of intelligent life on Mars that a French prize offered to the first person to contact extraterrestrials excluded the Red Planet. Martians were assumed to be too easy to locate!

By the 1930s, astronomers had determined that conditions on Mars were probably too harsh for the survival of anything but simple plants and animals, but the belief in Martians was too deeply embedded in the public mind to be discarded so easily. An example of how people confused fact and fiction concerning the Red Planet occurred in 1938, when the H. G. Wells novel *The War of the Worlds* was dramatized over the radio. Although it was clearly stated that the program was merely a fictional story, many listeners dashed frantically into the streets to escape the Martian "Heat-Rays," and a few people were hospitalized for shock and hysteria.

When reports of "flying saucers" (also called *unidentified flying objects*) increased in the 1950s, it was widely believed that they were spacecraft from Mars. The 1950s and 1960s were also the golden age of "Martian movies," which generally featured hostile and hideous aliens. In those years, exhibits about life on Mars were a standard feature of school science fairs. In 1958, I titled my eighth-grade science fair project "Is There Life on Mars?" but my teacher convinced me to change it to "There Is Life on Mars!" because so many scientists of the time believed the planet had vegetation. Thanks to Mr. Clark, I've been waiting to use the title "Is There Life on Mars?" for forty years.

In 1964, the United States launched the first of several probes that approached and eventually landed on the Red Planet. Photographs taken by the probes showed that Mars is a dry, cold world that seems to have no advanced forms of life. Yet the pictures also revealed that, long ago, Mars had flowing water and was warmer than it is now. There is a possibility that, back when its conditions were more conducive to life as we know it, the Red Planet was home to plants, animals, and even intelligent creatures.

The Red Planet reentered the public spotlight in 1996 when a team of scientists claimed that a rock from Mars contained fossils of tiny Martian organisms. Despite inconclusive evidence, headlines proclaiming LIFE ON MARS! appeared. Scientists speculated that if Mars once had microbes, the odds were increased that it also had more advanced life. Some scientists suggested that, through an interesting process, *we* might actually be Martians.

There seems to be only one way to find out whether Mars has ever had life. We must explore the planet. The United States is currently sending robotic spacecraft to Mars in preparation for the first human expedition to the Red Planet. One day early in the twenty-first century, explorers will land on Mars and search for signs of life, past and present. Then we may at last answer a question that has intrigued people for ages: Is there life on Mars?

D. B. F.
Evanston, Illinois
March 1, 1998

Mars and Ancient People

♂ **"Today few city-bred** children have any conception of the glories of the heavens," Percival Lowell wrote in 1906. Increased pollution and the growth of cities have made his words even truer today. Only by journeying to some place far from the smog and lights of civilization can we appreciate the full splendor of the night sky.

When we observe the heavenly bodies from a remote vantage point, we can imagine how our ancestors felt when they saw the same objects. One object especially would have attracted their attention, for at times it provided enough light for people to see at night. We call this huge, brilliant sphere that seems to continually change shape the Moon.

Once the Moon sets, we can understand the terror that the darkness must have held for early people. With no Moon, the only light came from the fires flickering in people's caves and the thousands of points of light in the sky, most of which seem to twinkle. The ancients observed that the twinkling objects remained in the same positions relative to one another, and imagined that groups of them formed pictures of such things as bears, a hunter, and a dog. We call the twinkling objects *stars,* and the imaginary star pictures *constellations.*

On certain nights, we might also notice several heavenly bodies that puzzled prehistoric observers. They resemble stars, yet instead of twinkling, they shine more steadily; and instead of remaining in fixed positions relative to the stars, they seem to wander through the constellations. We call these objects *planets,* from an ancient Greek word meaning "wanderers." Early people saw five planets of differing colors in the night sky: orange, white, red, yellow, and gold. All five of these planets are magnificent, but if the Red Planet is visible when we are stargazing, we can appreciate why ancient people found it especially intriguing. It resembles a droplet of blood, a substance associated with life and death.

We know that prehistoric people observed the sky, for we have found carved bones on which they recorded the Moon's cycles, stone monuments with which they monitored the Sun's movements, and pictures of stars on cave walls. They left no written records, however; so for the most part, we can only make educated guesses about what they thought of the heavenly bodies. Only after human beings invented writing approximately 5,000 years ago did people in many parts of the world write descriptions of their astronomical beliefs.

The Babylonians, an ancient people of what is now Iraq, believed that several of their gods sometimes took the form of the Sun, Moon, and five known planets. Because there were seven of these special objects, the Babylonians divided the week into seven days, a custom that survives today. According to the Babylonians, each of the seven days was influenced by one of the special objects. The bloodred planet reminded them of war, so the Babylonians called it *Nergal,* for their god of war and death. An ancient Babylonian text reads: "When Nergal is dim, good luck follows. When it is bright, disaster occurs." Nergal's special day was Tuesday. Priests who were supposed to prevent Nergal from causing trouble met on Tuesdays, dressed in red, and smeared themselves with blood.

To the ancient Egyptians, the Red Planet was one of the forms assumed by Horus, a god with a bird's head and a man's body. The ancient Jewish people believed that each planet ruled a part of the human body, a day of the week, and a letter of the alphabet. They thought the Red Planet influenced the right ear, Tuesday, and the Hebrew letter *daleth*. The Chinese called the Red Planet *Huo Xing,* the Fire Star, while Central American Indians called it *Macamil Kvku,* the Bright Red Star.

In ancient Persia (now Iran), the Red Planet embodied Pahlavani Siphir, the Sky Warrior. To the Greeks, the planet was a shape assumed by their war god, Ares. The Romans originated the names by which the planets are still known. The fast-moving orange planet that never strays far from the Sun they named Mercury, for their messenger god who sped along on magic sandals. The planet that looked as white as a cloud they named Venus, for their goddess of love and beauty. The Romans named the yellow planet Jupiter, for their king of the gods, and the golden planet Saturn, for Jupiter's father. They named the reddish planet Mars, for their god of war.

The name *Mars* has influenced our language and calendar. Several kinds of fighting are called the *martial* arts, a word from Latin (the language of the ancient Romans), meaning "of Mars." The boys' names Mark, Martin, and Marcus, and the girls' names Marcia, Marsha, and Marcy mean "belonging to Mars" and also come from Latin. Centuries ago, armies suspended wars in the wintertime because of the hazards of cold weather. Combat resumed when the snow melted, which is why we call the first month of spring *March,* in honor of the Roman war god, Mars. The ancient Romans also celebrated March 1 as New Year's Day. The custom of beginning the year in the month of March was maintained by much of the world until recent centuries. People in the thirteen British colonies that later became the United States celebrated March 25 as New Year's Day until 1752.

The Romans called the third day of the week *Dies Martis*—Latin for the "Day of Mars." The name has remained similar in several lan-

gives: Will roughness, strength, for-
titude, boldness, passion
likes: Struggle, animals
favours: Officers, surgeons, engineers
rules over: Aries Υ (practice, matter)
and Scorpion ♏ (theory, morals).

MARS
'INFORTUNA MINOR'

Colour: Red   Tone: D
Number: 9   Metal: Iron
            Jewel: Garnet
Virtue: Softness — Sense: Palate
Day: Tuesday (dies Martis)
Elements: Fire and water

Mars, the Roman god of war

guages that evolved from Latin. The third day of the week is *Mardi* in French, *Martedi* in Italian, *Martes* in Spanish, and *Marti* in Romanian. In English it is *Tuesday,* for Tiw, an old English god of war.

So that astronomers need not write out its whole name, each planet has a symbol. Mars's symbol is ♂, representing a shield and spear, and Venus's is ♀, showing the goddess's mirror. These emblems have entered into wider use, for scientists employ ♂ as a symbol for males (boys, men, and male animals), and ♀ for females (girls, women, and female animals).

People often wonder: Did the ancients really believe that heavenly bodies were gods? Apparently they did and they didn't. Their writings show that, while claiming that celestial bodies were deities, ancient people (especially scientifically minded individuals) also considered them to be merely objects in the sky. Yet even then they maintained many ideas that we now know to be false.

The prevailing view was that the Earth was the center of creation and that it stood motionless while the stars and planets, which were perhaps the size of marbles, circled above it. If you spend the entire night observing the sky, you can see how this erroneous idea originated. The

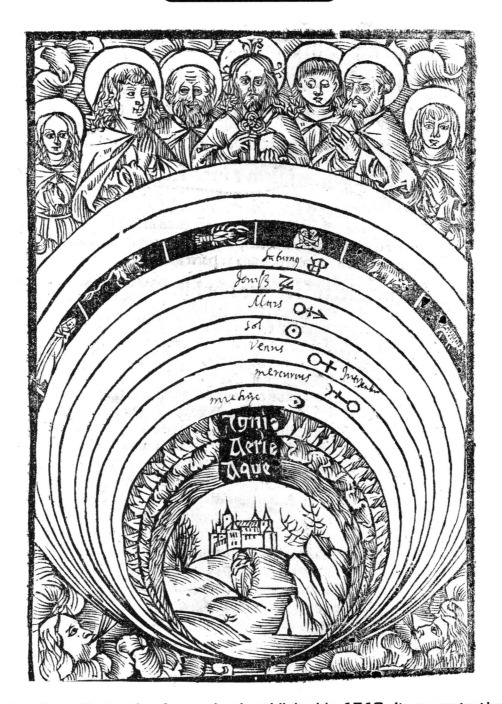

This is an illustration from a book published in 1513. It presents the
false view that Earth is the center of the Universe. Other objects in
the Solar System are shown orbiting Earth, which is represented as
the globe with the castle in it at bottom.

heavenly bodies *do* appear to circle above us as they rise in the east, arc across the sky, and set in the west. Furthermore, the stars and planets *do* seem to be much smaller than the Earth—unless you understand their immense distances from us.

Whether pictured as gods or as tiny objects, the planets were thought by ancient people to be incapable of supporting intelligent life. For how could creatures like ourselves live on a god or survive on an object as small as a marble?

Not until people began to understand the true nature of the Universe would they consider the possibility of life on Mars and the other planets.

two

Mars Is a World!

♂ **During the Middle Ages** (approximately A.D. 400-1400), the belief in a single God spread. Although the Roman names for the planets were retained, the ancient ideas about the numerous planet-gods faded. Yet they didn't completely die out, as shown by several pseudosciences (false sciences) that live on even today.

Astrology is a pseudoscience founded on the notion that heavenly bodies have personalities much like those of the ancient gods and that their positions in the sky help shape people's lives. Astrology should never be confused with astronomy, which is the scientific study of heavenly bodies. Probably no present-day astronomer believes in astrology, and astronomers tend to feel insulted when people mistakenly refer to them as astrologers.

In the Middle Ages, though, astronomy and astrology were closely intertwined. Throughout much of the world, the main reason people studied the night sky was to try to predict future events based on planet and star positions.

Illustration from an astrological book dating from 1484, showing Mars (at top) beaming his evil influence down upon Jupiter and Saturn

According to astrologers, each planet emits certain force fields of influence. Mars became associated with wars and other calamities—the same type of events the god was believed to influence in ancient times. Other qualities associated with the Red Planet were strength, energy, anger, the desire for power, and an impulse toward exploration and discovery. A child believed to be born under the influence of Mars might be expected to become a great soldier, a daring explorer, or, if lacking a healthy outlet for his or her aggressiveness, a murderer.

Palmistry is another false science based on the idea that the personalities of heavenly bodies influence our lives. However, palm readers claim that we need only study the lines, marks, and shapes on our hands to learn what the planet-gods have in store for us. For example, in palmistry, the little finger is the "Mercury finger" and the index finger the "Jupiter finger." In the middle of the palm is a flat area called the Plain of Mars, and below the little finger on the edge of the palm is a fleshy area known as the Mount of Mars. People with well-developed Plains and Mounts of Mars are called *Martians* in palmistry and are thought to have strong tempers and a love of competition and battle. [Figure 1]

By the end of the Middle Ages, people still believed that a Universe of tiny stars and planets circled our motionless Earth. The man who overturned this idea was born in what is now Toruń, Poland, on February 19, 1473. In his own time, Nicolaus Copernicus was best known as a canon (an official specializing in the Catholic Church's legal code) and as a physician. He also had a passion for astronomy. He could not view the planets close-up, for telescopes did not yet exist, but he used simple instruments to measure planetary positions.

Copernicus tackled an old astronomical problem. Now and then, Jupiter, Saturn, and, most noticeably, Mars make backward loops in the sky. The ancient Greeks explained this *retrograde motion* by asserting that, besides orbiting Earth in large circles, the planets sometimes travel backward in small circles known as *epicycles*. This idea was still accepted in Copernicus's time.

Copernicus rejected the epicycles idea, as well as the entire theory of an Earth-centered Universe. Earth, he argued, is a planet, the same as Mercury, Venus, Mars, Jupiter, and Saturn, and it resembles them in such important ways as size and motion. The planets all orbit the Sun, but Earth does so faster than Mars. When Earth overtakes Mars, the Red Planet appears to move backward, just as a person walking in the same direction as you but not as fast can appear to be moving backward. The nightly east-west movement of the stars and planets is another illusion, Copernicus concluded, caused by the fact that Earth spins like a top.

Copernicus presented his theory in *Concerning the Revolutions of the Heavenly Spheres,* a book readers found disturbing. If Copernicus was right (which he was), then Earth was not as important as people had thought. Moreover, if the other planets were worlds like Earth, why couldn't they, too, have intelligent life? Readers were also shocked that Copernicus had challenged the established Church view of an Earth-centered Universe. As a Church official, he might have been tortured or put to death for casting doubt on its teachings, but he was beyond earthly punishment. On May 24, 1543, just hours after being shown the first printed copy of his book, Nicolaus Copernicus died of natural causes at the age of seventy.

A few people accepted the *Copernican system* (the idea that the

Nicolaus Copernicus

Earth orbits the Sun instead of vice versa) immediately, but most people were hesitant, especially since religious leaders forbade such ideas. The Italian astronomer Giordano Bruno became a tragic example of the

danger of defying Church leaders. Bruno spoke in support of Copernicus and declared in a book: "There are numberless other Earths cir-
cling their suns, no worse and no less inhabited than this globe of
ours." For his unorthodox views, Bruno was burned to death in Rome,
Italy, on February 17, 1600. [Figure 2]

In 1608, Hans Lippershey of The Netherlands placed lenses on opposite ends of a tube and built the first telescope. The next year,
Galileo Galilei of Italy made a telescope and became the first astronomer to study the heavens with the new invention. When he aimed
his telescope at Jupiter, Galileo was amazed to see four moons orbiting
"the Giant Planet." As the moons traveled about Jupiter, Galileo realized he was seeing proof that all heavenly bodies do not orbit Earth.
Galileo wrote a book supporting the Copernican system. In 1633, he
was arrested and brought before officials in Rome. To keep from following in Giordano Bruno's footsteps, the sixty-nine-year-old scientist
had to fall to his knees and say that the Copernican system was false.

The facts couldn't be suppressed forever, though. As telescopes became more commonplace, people saw for themselves that Copernicus
had discovered the truth. By the year 1700, astronomers understood
these basic facts about the Universe:

*Throughout space are many millions of huge, hot balls of gas
called stars, which generate heat and light and appear to
twinkle as we view them through our atmosphere. The constellations barely change over time because their stars are so
far away that their motion appears slight to us. One star, the
Sun, shines big and bright in our daytime sky because it is
relatively nearby. The Sun and all the smaller bodies that
orbit it, including the planets, comprise what we call the
Solar System. The planets obtain heat and light from the
Sun and appear to shine rather steadily, and they seem to
move through the constellations because they are close to us*

compared to the background stars. As our Earth proves, planets can support life. Much as the planets orbit the Sun, smaller bodies called moons orbit some planets. Earth's Moon appears huge in our night sky because it is the heavenly body nearest to us. [Figure 3]

Once they realized that the other planets were worlds, astronomers began to speculate about their being inhabited. Christiaan Huygens [HY-gunz], an astronomer of the 1600s from The Netherlands, argued that Mercury, Venus, Mars, Jupiter, and Saturn were all home to intelligent beings. William Herschel, a German-English astronomer who discovered the seventh planet, Uranus, in 1781, was even more optimistic. Herschel proclaimed that intelligent life could be found on just about every heavenly body, even the Sun! In the early 1800s, the German scientist Franz von Paula Gruithuisen claimed that he had observed a ruined city on the Moon. Gruithuisen theorized that harsh conditions had forced the Selenites, as he called the Moon's inhabitants, to abandon their city and move underground.

Mars was believed to be the world most likely to have beings like ourselves. The more that was learned about Mars, the more it seemed to resemble Earth. In 1659, Christiaan Huygens made the first detailed drawing of Mars. Through his telescope, Huygens observed a large Y-shaped area on the planet that became known as the Syrtis Major, which means "Great Wetland" in Latin. Astronomers believed that the Syrtis Major and Mars's other dark greenish areas were water, which is an essential ingredient for life on Earth.

Each planet spins on an imaginary line called its *axis*. As a result of Earth's spinning, we have day and night, and heavenly bodies appear to rise in the east and set in the west. Earth spins, or rotates, once in 23 hours and 56 minutes—an Earth-day. By timing how long the Syrtis Major took to complete one spin, Christiaan Huygens figured the length of a Mars-day to be "24 Earth-hours." His result was close to the actual figure of 24 hours and 37 minutes, which is nearly the same length as an Earth-day.

In 1666, the Italian-French astronomer Giovanni Domenico Cassini described seeing white areas around Mars's North and South Poles. Mars's *polar caps,* as they became known, were assumed to be snow and ice, as are found around Earth's North and South Poles.

Each planet's axis is tilted at a certain angle. Earth's $23\frac{1}{2}$-degree tilt determines that most parts of the world have four seasons—summer, fall, winter, and spring. During the 1780s, William Herschel measured Mars's axial tilt at about 25 degrees—remarkably close to that of Earth. This showed that Mars might have four seasons just like our planet. Each Martian season would be about twice as long as an Earth-

season, though, because Mars takes nearly twice as long as Earth to orbit the Sun and therefore has a year nearly twice as long as ours.

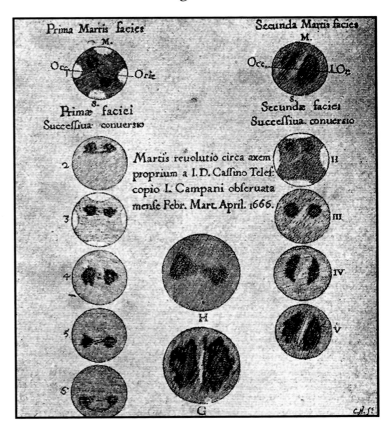

In addition to water, advanced life-forms (at least on Earth) require gases that they can breathe. Herschel observed what he called "clouds and vapors" on Mars, and he concluded that the planet's atmosphere was much like ours. Our world and the Red Planet were found to be similar in other ways. Earth and Mars are neighbors, the third and fourth planets from the Sun, which they orbit at average distances of 93 million miles

Drawings of Mars made by Giovanni Domenico Cassini in 1666

and 142 million miles, respectively. At its closest, Mars approaches within 35 million miles of Earth—closer to us than any other planet except Venus. Earth and Mars were also found to be comparable in size, with diameters of nearly 8,000 and about 4,200 miles, respectively. Based on all the similarities he noted between Earth and Mars, William Herschel thought that the Martians "probably enjoy a situation similar in many respects to our own."

In 1840, the German astronomers Wilhelm Beer and Johann von Mädler published the first detailed map of Mars. Among his achievements, von Mädler showed that Gruithuisen's "ruined lunar city" was actually just a mountain range on the Moon. Yet he and Beer helped spread the belief in Martians. Their maps of Mars—showing polar caps, dark areas believed to be water, and light regions thought to be deserts and other land—resembled our own Earth more than any other planet.

Scientists began to think of ways to inform the Martians of our existence. One suggestion came from Carl Gauss, a German mathematician who in 1801 had helped discover Ceres, the largest of the asteroids (a swarm of miniature planetlike objects located between Mars and Jupiter). During the 1820s, Gauss proposed that a right triangle be created in Siberia, a sparsely populated region of Russia. So as to be visible through the Martians' telescopes, the triangle would have to be larger than a city. Broad rows of pine trees would form the triangle's borders, and enormous quantities of wheat would be grown to fill its insides. Gauss's plan was not attempted. Russia and many other countries have often suffered from famines—severe food shortages leading to mass starvation. The idea of growing huge quantities of wheat just to serve as a message to Mars—while millions of Earthlings starved—wasn't any more acceptable in the 1800s than it would be today.

In the early 1800s, Joseph von Littrow, director of the Vienna Observatory in Austria, suggested that a 20-mile-wide ditch be constructed in Africa's Sahara Desert. Fill this enormous canal with kerosene, Littrow advised, and set it ablaze. The fire would be visible to the Martians, who would know that it wasn't natural because of the straightness of the canal. Like the wheat-and-pine-tree triangle, this plan was never put into effect, for who wanted to dig an enormous canal, waste tremendous amounts of kerosene, and foul the air with smoke?

Another plan was to build a network of huge mirrors across Europe, then aim them so as to reflect the light of the Sun at Mars. Observing the sunlight flashed to them in repeated patterns, the Martians would know we were here. Charles Cros, a French scientist, suggested this idea during the 1870s, but European countries were too occupied with political affairs and warfare to cooperate on a plan to signal Mars.

Nevertheless, by 1875, most people were convinced that it was only a matter of time before we detected a message from the Martians or discovered a way to contact them. The few skeptics who predicted that interest in the Red Planet would fade were in for a surprise, for a mania for Martians such as the world had never seen was about to begin.

Comparison of Earth and Mars

	Earth	Mars
Average Distance from Sun	93 million miles	142 million miles
Average Speed in Orbiting Sun	18 ½ miles per second	14 ½ miles per second
Length of Year	365 ¼ Earth-days	687 Earth-days
Length of Day	23 hours, 56 minutes	24 hours, 37 minutes
Diameter	7,926 miles	About 4,200 miles
Number of Moons	1	2
Tilt of Axis	23 ½ degrees	25 degrees
Atmosphere	Nitrogen, oxygen, argon, and tiny amounts of other gases	Mostly carbon dioxide, with small amounts of water vapor and other gases
Temperatures	Average: 57°F	Highs: 60s°F Lows: about -220°F
Gravitation	2 ⅔ times that of Mars	⅜ that of Earth

three

The Red Planet's Moons and "Canals"

♂ **For years, people** joked that Jonathan Swift was a Martian. In 1726, this Irish author published *Gulliver's Travels,* a novel about Dr. Lemuel Gulliver's visits to strange lands. On one voyage, Dr. Gulliver visits the island of Laputa, whose inhabitants are skilled astronomers. Using telescopes "far excelling ours," Dr. Gulliver explains, "they have discovered two [moons] which revolve about Mars," the innermost in a period of 10 hours about 12,000 miles above the planet, and the outermost in 21½ hours about 20,000 miles from Mars.

One hundred and fifty-one years after *Gulliver's Travels* appeared, Asaph Hall was observing Mars through the 26-inch telescope of the United States Naval Observatory in Washington, D.C. Every two years, Mars and Earth approach relatively near each other in an occurrence known as an *opposition*—called that because Mars is then positioned opposite the Sun, with the Earth in the middle. In 1877, Mars underwent a *most favorable opposition*—an event that occurs every few oppositions when the planet makes its closest approach of about 35 million miles to Earth. Hall and other astronomers eagerly aimed their telescopes at Mars, for these close encounters when Mars appeared especially bright in the sky provided the best opportunities for viewing the Red Planet.

Ever since the invention of the telescope, astronomers had searched for moons (also called *natural satellites*) that might be orbiting Mars. They had not found any, which meant that Mars had no big, bright moons. Hall decided to use the 1877 encounter with Mars to hunt for small moons that might have eluded other observers. Night after night, he searched for dim moons near Mars. Finally, he told his wife, Angelina Stickney Hall, that he was giving up. Reportedly she answered: "Asaph, look one more night." He did, and on August 11, he discovered a tiny point of light near Mars. Before he could determine what it was, fog obscured his view.

Asaph Hall eagerly awaited the next night, but it was cloudy, as were the three subsequent nights. Finally, on August 16, the sky cleared, and Hall determined that the tiny object was a moon orbiting Mars. The following night, he found a second moon even closer to the Red Planet. The little moons Hall had discovered were named Phobos (meaning "fear") and Deimos (meaning "terror") for the mythological attendants of the war god Mars. Phobos, the inner moon, has a diameter of just 15 miles and orbits Mars at a distance of 5,800 miles every $7\frac{1}{2}$ hours. Deimos, the outer moon, has only a 6-mile diameter and orbits Mars at a distance of 14,600 miles once every 30 hours.

Upon learning of Hall's discovery, people realized that Jonathan Swift's *Gulliver's Travels* not only correctly predicted the number of moons around Mars, but it was near the mark in describing their distances and orbital periods around the Red Planet. How did Swift come so near the truth 151 years before the moons were discovered?

Some people said that Swift knew about Mars because he came from the planet. Others claimed that telescopes had existed long before the 1600s and that ancient people had seen many things supposedly "discovered" later, including Mars's moons. Today we discount both ideas as silly. In *Gulliver's Travels,* Swift pokes fun at some of the scientific ideas of his time. Some astronomers thought that each planet outward from Earth had twice as many moons as the planet before, meaning that Mars would have two moons, Jupiter four, Saturn eight, and so on. Swift seems to have accidentally stumbled upon some facts about Phobos and Deimos while criticizing this theory about a planet's number of moons. Although it happens to work for Mars, Jupiter actually has at least sixteen moons, while Saturn has more than twenty!

Another false idea of the past was that the greater a planet's distance from the Sun, the older it was. This belief resulted from an erroneous theory about the origin of our Solar System. Today's astronomers believe that the Solar System began as a single huge cloud of gas and dust about five billion years ago. The central region shrank, generating so much energy that it ignited a nuclear reaction and became the Sun. Meanwhile, particles in the rest of the cloud joined together to become the planets and their moons. *Meanwhile* is a key word in this "single-gas-cloud theory," which suggests that the Sun and planets all began close to the same time, so that one planet is not much different in age than another.

But in the 1800s, many scientists believed in the *nebular hypothesis.* Presented in 1796 by French mathematician Pierre-Simon de Laplace, it resembles the modern theory up to a point in that it suggests our Solar System began as a huge cloud of gas and dust. However, it goes on to propose that the planets did not form at about the same time as the Sun. Instead, they formed later, as the newborn Sun threw off rings of gas and dust that became the planets and their moons. The first rings the Sun shed became the outermost planets, and the last rings the innermost. If this were true, then the outermost were the oldest planets and the innermost the youngest.

The nebular hypothesis had implications for believers in extraterrestrials. Located closer to the Sun than is Earth, Venus was considered to be younger than our planet and therefore to have more primitive life. The first known dinosaur fossils were discovered on Earth in the early 1800s. Many people became convinced that Venus was similar to our Earth of ages past, with dinosaurs roaming its swamps and flying reptiles soaring through its skies. Perhaps Venus was even home to humanoids (meaning "humanlike creatures") who resembled lizards. Anyone could say the zaniest things about Venus without fear of being disproven. At times approaching within 26 million miles of Earth, Venus is the only planet that comes closer to us than Mars, but a perpetual veil of clouds prevents telescopes from revealing its surface.

Mars, on the other hand, was believed to have been formed before Earth, so that any Martian civilization would be older and more advanced than our own. With that in mind, astronomers of the late 1800s studied the Red Planet for evidence of a highly developed civilization. As a result of a misunderstanding involving a single word, many people thought that we discovered that evidence in 1877.

Giovanni Virginio Schiaparelli [ski-a-peh-REH-lee] was one of the astronomers scrutinizing Mars during that year's most favorable opposition. Born in Savigliano, Italy, in 1835, Schiaparelli discovered a new asteroid, Hesperia, when he was only twenty-six. He won prizes, became an expert on *comets* (objects that develop long, glowing tails when near the Sun) and *meteoroids* (pieces of stone or metal that flame across the sky when they burn up in Earth's atmosphere), and, at the age of twenty-seven, he was named director of Italy's Milan Observatory.

Schiaparelli was observing Mars

Giovanni Virginio Schiaparelli

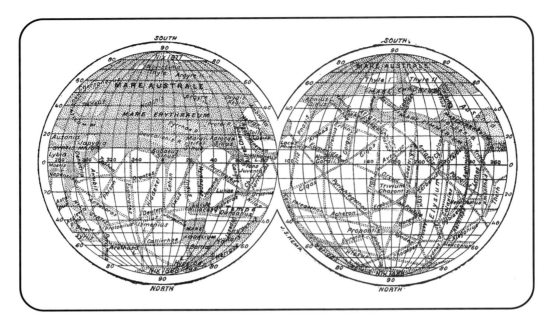

Charts of Mars by Schiaparelli showing the Martian canals

one night in 1877 when he saw something startling. A network of barely visible lines seemed to be crisscrossing the planet. The lines were so straight that they "appeared as though laid down by a ruler," he noted. Schiaparelli reported what he had seen, but he could offer no explanation for his observation. "We may designate them as *canali* although we do not yet know what they are," he wrote.

The word *canali* began a scientific battle, often called the "canals controversy," that raged for a century.

In Italian, *canali* can refer to "channels" or "canals"—two words with vastly different meanings. Generally "channels" refer to natural riverbeds, and "canals" to man-made waterways such as ship canals or irrigation ditches. By saying "we do not yet know what they are," Schiaparelli emphasized that he did not know whether the *canali* were natural or constructed by Martians. Most readers chose the more exciting possibility and assumed that Schiaparelli thought they were artificial. This was especially true in English-speaking lands, for *canali* is nearly the same as the English word *canals.*

Astronomers were less impressed than the public by Schiaparelli's reports. They didn't doubt his honesty, but they wanted proof that he hadn't been the victim of an optical illusion.

The sky can trick us in many ways. The "Moon illusion" is a famous example. You may have noticed that the Moon looks bigger and closer when rising or setting than it does when it is high in the sky. Although photographs show that the Moon is actually the same size regardless of its position in the sky, for reasons that scientists debate our brains perceive the Moon as being larger when it is just above the horizon. Were the lines Schiaparelli had described on Mars also an optical illusion?

The size of Schiaparelli's telescope increased the possibility that the lines or *canali* he described were an illusion. There are two main types of telescopes. Refracting telescopes (refractors) operate with lenses, while reflecting telescopes (reflectors) have mirrors. A telescope's size is measured by the diameter of its mirror or lens. Schiaparelli was using an 8¾-inch refractor—a relatively small telescope for a major observatory. In comparison, Asaph Hall's 26-inch refractor was three times that diameter. Why didn't Asaph Hall, or any other astronomer, see the *canali* that Schiaparelli observed in 1877? One possibility was that the "seeing" (quality of air) was better at Milan Observatory than elsewhere. In that case, a smaller telescope could reveal details invisible to a much larger instrument.

Not only did Schiaparelli continue to see the *canali*, but he reported that they began to change in astounding ways. During the 1879 opposition of the Red Planet, he discovered that one canal had developed a twin. Where there had been a single canal, there were now two, running parallel to each other. At the next opposition, in early 1882, he observed *twenty* examples of canals that had doubled. When other observers continued to search in vain for single canals, let alone doubles, Schiaparelli defended himself. "It is no optical illusion," he wrote. "I am absolutely sure of what I have observed."

In April 1886, nine years after Schiaparelli had first seen the *canali,* Henri Perrotin and Louis Thollon were observing Mars through a 15-inch refractor at Nice Observatory in France when they saw both single and double canals. After that, the list of canal spotters grew with each opposition. In 1892, William H. Pickering, an American astronomer working at Harvard University's observatory at Arequipa, Peru, saw the canals. "Numerous so-called canals exist upon the planet, substantially as drawn by Professor Schiaparelli," Pickering wrote. "Some of them are only a few miles in breadth."

Despite the canal observers' testimony, many scientists still believed that the phenomenon was an illusion, or that the markings were real but had a natural explanation. One theory was that Mars's surface had developed cracks similar to those on an old vase. As late as 1893, even the discoverer of the canals wasn't quite ready to say that Martians existed. "Some see in [the canals] the work of intelligent beings," Schiaparelli cautiously wrote in a scientific journal. "I am very careful not to combat this supposition, which includes nothing impossible."

Camille Flammarion was a notable exception to the rule of caution regarding the canals. In 1862 this colorful French astronomer published *La Pluralité des Mondes Habités (The Numerous Inhabited Worlds),* a book expressing his view that the Universe teems with intelligent life. During the 1880s, a wealthy amateur stargazer gave Flammarion an estate near Paris that had once been frequented by France's King Louis XIV. There Flammarion established an observatory where he studied Mars. Flammarion painted the ceiling of his living quarters pale blue, with fleecy clouds, and decorated his twelve dining room chairs with pictures of the twelve constellations of the Zodiac, the belt across the sky through which the planets move.

In 1892, Flammarion published the first volume of *La Planète Mars et ses Conditions d'Habitabilité (The Planet Mars and Its Conditions for Habitability),* in which he proclaimed the likelihood of Martians. "Mars appears habitable to the same degree as the Earth," he wrote. "It

Camille Flammarion

is older, and so its humanity could be more advanced than ourselves." He continued: "The climate and conditions for life on Mars appear to be similar enough to Earth that species slightly different from ours could live there."

Even in the planet's reddish areas—thought by most astronomers to be deserts—Flammarion saw life. Red plants might cause the color, he explained, and then he asked his readers: "Why, we may ask, is not the Martian vegetation green? Why should it be? There is no reason to regard the [Earth's vegetation] as typical in the Universe." Flammarion told a *New York Times* interviewer: "I would like to go to Mars. No doubt the floods that cover the plains every Summer would bother me at first, but one can get used to anything, and perhaps the Martians are amphibious, or know how to fly just as easily as we can walk on dry land."

His outspoken manner made Flammarion a handy target for those who were skeptical about life on Mars. A newspaper published a cartoon showing him with Martians, along with the caption: CAMEL FLIMFLAMMARION ANNOUNCES THAT HE HAS DISTINCTLY SEEN PEOPLE SWIMMING IN THE CANALS OF MARS. Often he answered his critics with humor. In 1894, after an article appeared in the *Publications of the Astronomical Society of the Pacific* asserting that "the Earth [is] the most important of the planets, and the center of creation," Flammarion wrote a reply under the name "A Citizen of Mars." Pretending to be a Martian, he mocked the writer of the earlier article by claiming that "our Mars [is] the most important of the planets, and the center of creation." The "Citizen of Mars" declared that life couldn't exist on Earth, because it was closer to the Sun than Mars and therefore must be too hot.

But the flamboyant Camille Flammarion would not be the main spokesperson for Martians much longer. As the Red Planet swung toward opposition in the autumn of 1894, a new astronomer was about to become the leading advocate for intelligent life on Mars.

four

The "Lowellization" of Mars

♂ **The date is** October 1906, and, as has been occurring twice every day, a huge crowd is pouring into Boston's Huntington Hall. Although the hall has a thousand seats, tickets are in such demand that many people must be turned away. This is not unusual for these lectures, which feature Percival Lowell speaking about life on Mars.

To appreciate the interest Lowell generated, we must remember that in 1906, people did not have the kinds of entertainment we enjoy today. Television did not yet exist. Guglielmo Marconi had invented radio in 1895, but the first regular broadcasts did not occur until 1920. "Flickers" (as movies were called) were still in their infancy and attracted small audiences by today's standards. Professional basketball and football were not yet established, and even the "national pastime," baseball, was not nearly as popular as it is today. When the people of 1906 sought entertainment, they went to plays, concerts, circuses, and lectures.

Once the Huntington Hall audience is seated, the speaker enters—

an impeccably dressed, debonair, mustachioed man of fifty-one who carries a walking cane for flair. He is Percival Lowell, and he is about to explain his views about the Martians and the canals they have constructed.

Lowell was born in Boston, Massachusetts, on the Day of Mars in the Month of Mars—Tuesday, March 13, 1855. He belonged to one of America's most prominent families. In the early 1800s, Francis Cabot Lowell had helped establish the family fortune by founding the country's modern cotton industry. Percival's cousin, James Russell Lowell, was a poet and also served as a United States minister to Spain and England. Percival's sister, Amy Lowell, became a Pulitzer Prize-winning poet, while their brother, Abbott Lawrence Lowell, became the president of Harvard University, the nation's oldest college.

Perhaps because he grew up in the midst of war, Percival Lowell hated fighting and conflict throughout his life. The Civil War broke out between the Northern and Southern states when he was six. Three

Percival Lowell

years later, his family embarked on an extended European trip. While the Lowells were in Germany in 1866, Europe's Seven Weeks' War began. One skirmish was fought in the town where Percival and his family were staying.

For much of his two years in Europe, Percival attended school in France and Switzerland, where classes were taught in French. By the time the Lowells sailed for home, Percival had an ability to learn languages quickly, a love for travel, and an appreciation for other cultures.

Back in the States, Percival's family settled in Brookline, Massachusetts, outside of Boston. At about the age of twelve, Percival became enchanted with astronomy and read every book he could find on the subject. His father gave him a 2¼-inch refracting telescope, with which Percival set up a little observatory on the flat roof of his house. He especially enjoyed viewing Mars, which even through his small telescope revealed its red surface, green patches, and white polar caps.

In the fall of 1872, Percival enrolled at Harvard, where famed mathematician and astronomer Benjamin Peirce considered him one of the most brilliant students he'd ever had. Professor Peirce advised him to become an astronomer, and when Percival spoke at his own graduation in 1876, he chose the nebular hypothesis as his topic. He was expected to work in the family businesses for a few years, though, and he also wanted to travel, so astronomy would remain in the background for nearly twenty years.

For several years, Percival Lowell ran a cotton mill, managed trust funds, and made such wise investments that, by 1883, when he was twenty-eight, he never had to work again if he chose. Yet having money was merely a starting point for the Lowells. As his father had directed Percival in his youth: In exchange for having every advantage, he must devote his life to something "of real significance."

Among his talents, Percival Lowell was a gifted writer. Americans of his time knew little of the Far East, a region that includes Japan, Korea, and China. He decided to visit the Far East and describe it for the English-speaking world. He spent ten years traveling in the Far East, interspersed with occasional visits back home. Books he wrote about his Asian experiences include *Chöson—The Land of the Morning Calm: A Sketch of Korea* and *Soul of the Far East*, about Japan.

Having seen so much of his own world, Percival Lowell began to think about worlds beyond. On his final visit to Japan in 1891, he brought along a 6-inch refracting telescope. He found Saturn's rings and Mars so intriguing that, by the time he returned home in late 1893, he had reached a decision about his lifework. Giovanni Schiaparelli, now fifty-eight years old and having vision problems, could no longer lead the way in studying Mars. Camille Flammarion was fifty-one years old. A younger astronomer was needed with the keen eyesight and energy required to unravel the mystery of the Martian canals. Percival Lowell decided to devote himself to the Red Planet.

He would begin by building the greatest observatory on Earth for studying Mars, at a location where the "seeing" was outstanding. He was determined to construct his observatory in a matter of months, in time for the opposition in the fall of 1894.

Lowell hired astronomers William H. Pickering and Andrew E. Douglass to help establish his observatory, and he considered such sites as South America's Andes Mountains, Algeria, France, Mexico, and the Southwestern United States. Pickering thought Arizona was a likely area, so Lowell lent Douglass his 6-inch refractor and told him to roam the territory to find a locale with great seeing. In the spring of 1894, Douglass made tests at Tombstone, Tucson, Phoenix, and other Arizona locations. He especially liked the seeing in a mountainous area of northern Arizona near the young town of Flagstaff. On April 16, Lowell sent Douglass a letter declaring: FLAGSTAFF IT IS!

It was a fine choice. Not only was the seeing good around Flagstaff, but with clouds present only 10 percent of the time, Arizona has the nation's clearest skies. The Arizona Territory's population was just 100,000, so pollution and city lights posed no problems. Also, the site was in one of the world's most scenic regions, near such natural wonders as Meteor Crater, a hole nearly a mile across made thousands of years ago when a huge object from space crashed to Earth; the Painted Desert, with its colorful sands and rocks; the Petrified Forest, where trees turned to stone long ago; and the famous, mile-deep Grand Canyon.

The observatory was begun in late April 1894. Workmen constructed the buildings and a road up "Mars Hill," as the site became known. (To this day, Lowell Observatory's address is 1400 West Mars Hill Road.) An 18-inch refractor was shipped in, and later a 24-inch refractor and a 40-inch reflector were installed. Percival Lowell arrived by train on May 28, and on June 1, 1894—just six weeks after the groundbreaking—Lowell Observatory opened.

Sleeping by day, Lowell spent long nights at the telescope. At the time photographing the planets was of little value, because few details could be captured. Astronomers drew pictures of the planets. In the observatory's first year of operation, Lowell and his assistants made nearly a thousand drawings of Mars.

The men were astonished by what they saw. Schiaparelli had detected about 100 canals. Lowell and his staff counted approximately *500* canals, which averaged about 1,000 miles in length. Lowell measured one canal at 3,540 miles—only a few hundred miles less than the planet's entire diameter. He agreed with Schiaparelli that some canals were double, "like the twin rails of a railroad track," and he also observed changes in the canals over time. "At certain seasons they cease to exist," he noted, only to become visible again in the Martian springtime.

William H. Pickering made a further discovery, confirmed by Lowell. Approximately 200 dark, roundish spots dotted the Red Planet. These "oases," as Lowell called them, were located in places where several canals converged. Lowell compared the oases to "hubs" of wheels, and the canals to the "spokes" radiating from them.

What did all of this mean? Within a year of opening his observatory, Lowell wrote four articles about the Red Planet that appeared in the *Atlantic Monthly* in May, June, July, and August of 1895. These articles were the basis for his first astronomy book, *Mars,* published that same year. The book had a tremendous impact, for it proposed a fascinating theory about the Martians.

Lowell claimed that Mars was "a world much older than the Earth."

Percival Lowell at the telescope

Over time, it had lost much of its atmosphere, but its remaining air was similar to Earth's and sufficient to support life. Mars also had an "astonishingly mild" climate, Lowell asserted, with average temperatures actually warmer than Earth's. "It is almost perpetually fine weather on our neighbor in space," he declared. "A cloud is an event on Mars, a rare and unusual phenomenon."

But few clouds means little or no rain. Moreover, because of Mars's advanced age, much of its original water had dried up, "retreating through cracks and caverns into its interior." With a "water supply now exceedingly low," the planet had become mostly desert. Fortunately, the Martians, whose civilization was far older and more advanced than ours, had given up war and learned to cooperate. They had dug an elaborate system of irrigation canals through which they pumped water from their North and South Poles to all parts of their thirsty planet.

"The visible development of the canal system follows the melting of the polar snows," when the water pumping began, Lowell explained. The canals themselves were too thin to be visible in our telescopes, so what astronomers actually saw were rows of crops growing along the canals. The Syrtis Major and other large dark greenish areas were not seas, but vast regions of vegetation. The dark spots were cities, which were built where several canals converged because their inhabitants needed large amounts of water. The double canals puzzled Lowell, but he soon formed a theory about them, too. When one canal could not convey enough water to a region, the Martians opened a second canal, parallel to the first.

What did the Martians look like? Lowell saved this topic for the end of his four-part magazine series and the last few pages of *Mars*. "To talk of Martian beings is not to mean Martian men," he wrote, for they probably "would strike us as exquisitely grotesque." For one thing, they were likely to be much larger than ourselves. Mars is smaller than Earth, with three-eighths of our planet's gravity, so that a 100-pound Earthling would weigh only 38 pounds on Mars. This meant that "Nature could afford there to build her inhabitants on three times the scale she does on Earth." A Martian was probably about 20 feet tall, Lowell figured, and "if on Earth, would weigh 27 times as much as the human

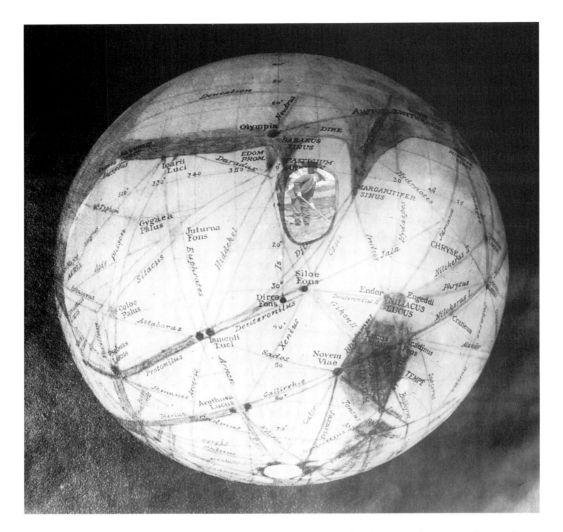

This model of Mars made by Percival Lowell shows the canals and oases. Lowell's staff pasted a picture of Lowell gardening onto the model and presented it to him as a gift for his fiftieth birthday in 1905.

being," or about 4,000 pounds. This would make the average Martian a little taller and heavier than a giraffe. Lowell also concluded that Martians had fifty times the strength of human beings, which meant that canal building was much easier for them than it would be for us.

Readers gobbled up Lowell's theory. People were awed that we might have superintelligent giants as interplanetary neighbors. To a world constantly at war, the idea that Martians had learned to live in peace provided hope. At a time when the American West needed water to develop cities and farms, Mars's global canal system seemed to show what irrigation could achieve. Lowell's theory may have helped inspire the 1902 Reclamation Act, a U.S. government program that built irrigation projects throughout the West. Also, in an era when human beings wanted to reach our North Pole (achieved in 1909) and South Pole (achieved in 1911), Lowell's assertion that the Martians had learned to tap their polar resources was exciting.

Percival Lowell continued to study Mars over the next several years. By the early 1900s, he was widely considered to be the leading expert on the planet, with which he was so closely identified that he signed some letters "Mars." Even in love notes to lady friends, he made reference to his reputation as an expert on Mars. "The Messenger from Mars has received [your] message," he wrote in one note, and he signed others "with the compliments of a Martian" and "A Martian Ambassador on Earth." He also wrote more books—*Mars and Its Canals* in 1906 and *Mars as the Abode of Life* in 1908—which elaborated upon his earlier ideas. He was so interesting a writer that magazines competed for his articles, and he was so charming a speaker that he attracted crowds wherever he lectured in the United States and Europe. Describing Lowell's effect on audiences, a journalist wrote: "This reporter has met many of the so-called great men of his time, but none with a more potent personal quality than Percival Lowell. One felt it before, or almost before, he entered the room. It was as if one had been suddenly deposited in a powerful magnetic field."

Fortunately, his "magnetism" didn't swell his head. When uninvited visitors came to Mars Hill, "Uncle Percy" (as the Lowell Observatory staff calls him to this day) showed them the Red Planet through his telescope. At Christmastime, he dressed as Santa Claus, welcomed local children to his observatory, and gave them presents and candy. He was also patient with writers, explaining his ideas to them in simple terms. As a result, reporters swarmed around him, publishing articles with such titles as MARS INHABITED, SAYS PROFESSOR LOWELL and WHO DUG THE CANALS ON MARS?

A typical article about Lowell appeared in the December 9, 1906, *New York Times* under the title THERE IS LIFE ON THE PLANET MARS. Reporter Lilian Whiting prefaced her article with the teaser: "Professor Percival Lowell, Recognized as the Greatest Authority on the Subject, Declares There Can Be No Doubt That Living Beings Inhabit Our Neighbor World." Beneath a canal-covered map of Mars, Lowell's views were presented, ending with his assertion: "The only logical [explanation], is that the oases are great centers of population, that the canals are constructed by guiding intelligence, and that [the canals'] existence is an unanswerable and an absolute proof that there is conscious, intelligent, organic life on Mars." When he stated in *Scientific American* in October 1907 that the odds were "millions to one" in favor of intelligent life on Mars, and when he declared two years later that the Martians had built two new canals, nearly everyone accepted his opinions as gospel.

Nearly everyone. The doubters included many of Lowell's fellow astronomers. Unlike the public, which generally admired and respected Lowell, professional astronomers tended to view him as a hobbyist who had used his fortune to make himself the world's leading astronomical "star." Other astronomers were also jealous of him. While they published papers in obscure scientific journals and worked for years before gaining access to large telescopes, Lowell had his own observatory, wrote best-selling books, and delved into astronomy's most romantic topic: the search for extraterrestrial life.

Jealousy aside, Lowell's critics had two legitimate complaints. Astronomers usually check and recheck their data for years before announcing their results. Lowell had rushed *Mars* into print so soon after founding his observatory that it was clear he had been predisposed to see canals. Also, a number of respected and experienced astronomers observed Mars repeatedly and never once saw canals.

New York Times.

NEW YORK, FRIDAY, AUGUST 30, 1907.—SIXTEEN PAGES.   ONE

DREDS STORM BELLEVUE GATE

eeks Chauffeur Who Took rl He Had Run Over to Hospital.

LLAPSES FROM FRIGHT

Father Cries "Kidnapper" n He Sees Auto Driver Put Her In His Car.

ing and throwing stones and missiles hundreds of persons the main gate of Bellevue Hos-night in an attempt to attack L. Bender of 114 Washington arrytown, who a few moments d run over and seriously injured ieman, 13 years old, of 404 East ourth Street.

in an automobile, was crossing ourth Street at Second Avenue, min suddenly ran out into the front of his machine. She had len by a wagon until just the in-fore, and though Bender threw rakes it was too late, and the eel of the car struck the little cking her down.

g the car to a standstill, Bender as did two well-dressed women, ran to the injured girl, but with-ng her a glance the two women away, and were last seen board-rth-bound Second Avenue car.

time, shortly after 6 o'clock, the as crowded with men and women, sight of the injured girl roused fury. Her father, who had been in the front door of their home, d by one of the girl's playmates, had happened. He rushed to the ttime to see Bender, ignoring the pick the little girl up in his arms, on the rear seat of the car, and nop in himself. Misunderstanding on of the chauffeur, the father of shouted "Kidnapper!" The cry en up, and instantly there was a lurge after Bender's machine, already was speeding toward the hospital, Bellevue.

the mob was after him, and not unding the cause, Bender turned re power and shot away, arriving kate of the hospital hotly pursued. th enough time to spare. The mob lose behind, and the gatekeeper d the gate in their faces. ntly there arose a howl from the ted crowd and it surged against

WATTERSON'S PAPER BURNED.

Fire Early This Morning in the Courier-Journal Building.

LOUISVILLE, Ky., Friday, Aug. 30.— Fire started early this morning in the building of the Louisville Courier-Journal, of which Henry Watterson is editor. At 1 o'clock it seemed that the building was doomed. All the employes escaped.

SHUT OFF LA FOLLETTE.

Teachers Wouldn't Let Him Speak on Partisan Politics.

Special to The New York Times.
PITTSBURG, Aug. 29.—United States Senator Robert A. La Follette of Wiscon-sin, was prevented from discussing parti-san politics at the teachers' institute here this afternoon by Superintendent of Schools, Samuel Hamilton. Senator La Follette was scheduled to speak on "Rep-resentative Government."

Earlier in the day he had been re-quested to keep off of partisan politics, and in opening his speech he said:

"I have been warned not to be partisan in my speech here this afternoon, but I want to say to the superintendent and the officials of the institute just what I think."

Before he could get any further, Supt. Hamilton jumped up, and declared that the institute was no place for the discus-sion of politics, and that the Senator would have to eliminate any partisan talk. After a hurried conference between the Superintendent and the Senator, La Follette proceeded with his speech, which was rather tame.

$600,000 TIMES SQUARE DEAL.

Plot Sold for the Shanleys May Be for Theatre Site.

As the result of a $600,000 real estate deal closed yesterday, it is believed that Times Square is soon to have another large theatre.

The McVickar-Gaillard Realty Com-pany, as broker, has sold for Shanley Brothers the properties 1,555 Broadway and 203 to 217 West Forty-sixth Street. The Broadway lot measures 23.10 by 89 feet, while the eight houses at the rear, on the north side of Forty-sixth Street, cover a frontage of 130 feet.

Nothing as to the identity of the buyer could be learned yesterday from either the brokers or the sellers, but the combined properties make up a plot of the size and shape most in demand among theatre builders—that is, enough Broadway frontage to provide a suitable entrance connecting with a larger parcel of less valuable ground on a side street.

The entire plot has an area of about 16,000 feet, so that if a theatre is erected

MARS INHABITED, SAYS PROF. LOWELL

Declares the Planet to Be the Abode of Intelligent, Con-structive Life.

THE RECENT OBSERVATIONS

Changes in Canals Confirm Former Theory—Splendid Photographs Were Obtained.

Special Cable to THE NEW YORK TIMES.
LONDON, Aug. 29.—In answer to a request from the editor of Nature for an authoritative statement of the ob-servations of Mars made during the 1907 opposition, Prof. Percival Lowell communicates to that publication what he describes as "two or three of the most important results obtained."

He declares that the planet is at pres-ent the abode of intelligent, construct-ive life. The results obtained, writes Prof. Lowell, exceed what seemed likely in view of the unfavorable declination of the planet in a position so southern as to render it practically unobservable in England, France, or the northern part of the United States.

Prof. Lowell goes on to speak of the observations of the polar caps. He says that owing to the fact that observations were begun in March, three months and a half before the opposition, it was pos-sible to catch both caps at an inter-esting phase of their careers, the south-ern one at its maximum and the north-ern at its minimum extent. The mo-ment was more propitious than had ever been the case before at times at which the planet had been observed, because it was then upon an even keel as re-gards the earth, the Equator lying nearly in the plane of sight. The southern cap at this epoch stretched across 95 degrees of latitude, counting from one side of it to the other, and the northern only over 8 degrees. From that date the dwindling of the south-ern cap and the making of the north-ern were carefully watched in order to complete the confirmation of the curi-

REBUKE BY KING EDWAR

He Walks Out of a Cafe Owing Nature of the Performance

MARIENBAD, Aug. 29.—King has administered a rebuke to the of indelicate songs in places of amusement, and his action, which taken publicly, has created inter citement in Marienbad.

His Majesty entered a café t to-night, and, after listening to one items on the programme, he walk as a protest against the scandalo ure of the performance. A Vienne pany was playing. His Majesty v lowed by the Duke of Teck and th members of his suite, and all the icans and Englishmen present.

"This is horrible, appalling," s King to a member of his entoura, the accuracy of his description performance is admitted on every

YELLOW FEVER NEAR HA

It Appears at Campo, Across t from the City.

WASHINGTON, Aug. 29.—A ca from Havana to the Marine Service reports the appearance of fever at Campo, across the ba Havana.

There is one undoubted case an are other suspected cases.

Gov. Magoon to-day reported War Department that the yellor situation at Cienfuegos continued prove. The last soldier to have ease was discharged yesterday.

A "SPANISH PRISONER"

Seven Persons Arrested—Made in Fifteen Months.

Special Cable to THE NEW YORK LONDON, Aug. 29.—A telegra Madrid says that a gang of sev sons has been arrested for carr the "Spanish prisoner" fraud. In the last fifteen months th obtained $70,000.

WHITE CITY BURNING

Big Pleasure Resort at Cle Oplo, is in Flames.

Special to The New York Times CLEVELAND, Ohio, Aug. 29 City, a big pleasure resort near th is in flames.

Percival Lowell was widely quoted in the newspapers of his time. This article is from the August 30, 1907, *New York Times*.

Around the time that Lowell founded his observatory in 1894, sev-eral big telescopes went into operation, including Lick Observatory's 36-inch refractor in California and Yerkes Observatory's 40-incher (to this day the world's largest refractor) in Wisconsin. The eagle-eyed American astronomer Edward Emerson Barnard used both these instruments. He discovered sixteen comets, Jupiter's fifth moon, and "Barnard's star," but when he observed Mars, he saw no canals. "To save my soul, I can't believe in the canals," Barnard wrote. "I see details where some of [the canals are supposedly located], but they are not straight lines at all." Barnard predicted that one day the canals would be proved to be "a fallacy."

Several astronomers who for a time believed in the canals later changed their minds. While working as Flammarion's assistant, Eugene Michael Antoniadi reported seeing dozens of canals through a 9-inch refractor. In the early 1900s, Antoniadi used the far more powerful 33-inch refractor at Meudon Observatory near Paris, France, and became one of Lowell's harshest critics. When seeing was poor and the image of Mars was hazy, said Antoniadi, he sometimes thought he discerned the canals. But when seeing was excellent, the straight lines disappeared and turned into "a maze of knotted, irregular, chequered streaks and spots."

Partly because of criticism from other astronomers, Lowell suffered a mental breakdown in 1897. He spent a month in bed and did little work for more than three years. His brother-in-law, William Putnam, ran the observatory in his absence. When he returned to work in the spring of 1901, Lowell made a disturbing discovery. Andrew E. Douglass had complained to Putnam that Lowell was "unscientific" for claiming that Mars had intelligent life without providing sufficient evidence. Deeply wounded by this comment from a man who had helped him found the observatory, Lowell fired Douglass.

By this time, the "canal controversy" was raging. On one side were the "canalists" or "Lowellians"—people who believed in the canals and in Martians. They included perhaps a third of all astronomers, including Percival Lowell and Camille Flammarion, as well as nearly all of the public. Just how widespread the idea of Martians had become was demonstrated by a prize established around the year 1900. Frenchman Pierre Guzman believed in Flammarion's writings so passionately that he was certain humanity would soon contact Martians. After Guzman died, his family established the Pierre Guzman Prize, offering "the sum of 100,000 francs to whoever communicates with the inhabitants of a cosmic body other than the planet Mars." The family didn't think that the money, which would equal about $400,000 in today's U.S. dollars, should go to someone merely for contacting Martians, which was expected to happen momentarily.

Opposed to the canalists were the "anti-canalists" or "anti-Lowellians"—people who did not believe in canal-building Martians. This group included a small portion of the public and at least a third of all astronomers, including Barnard and Antoniadi. The remaining astronomers, including Schiaparelli and Pickering, believed that the *canali* existed but that they were not necessarily built by intelligent creatures.

Each side marshaled its arguments. No one accused Lowell of lying about the canals, for he had a reputation as a man of integrity, and, besides, many other people claimed to have seen the structures. Those who doubted the canals' existence generally felt that they were some type of optical illusion.

In 1903, English astronomer Edward Walter Maunder conducted a simple experiment. Maunder drew assorted smudges, squiggles, circles, dots, and dashes on a big piece of white paper. He hung his drawing in front of a classroom of thirteen-year-old students and asked them to sketch what they saw. Students toward the front tended to see separate details, but those farther back who couldn't see the picture well tended to connect the marks into thin, straight lines resembling the Martian canals. The anti-canalists concluded that our eyes and brains sometimes connect barely visible features into straight lines.

The anti-canalists also pointed out that Lowell's drawings of Mercury and Venus showed what looked like canals. Nearly everyone (except perhaps Flammarion) agreed that Mercury was too hot to have a canal-building civilization, while clouds prevented optical telescopes from revealing Venus's surface. This seemed to be a clue that Lowell's eyes played tricks on him and that, for some reason, he imagined he saw straight lines on objects where there were none.

Writing in the February 1907 *Catholic World* magazine, Father George Searles summarized the anti-canalists' viewpoint. Everything on the Red Planet could be explained "without any idea of Mars being inhabited," Father Searles wrote. "It seems clear that [Lowell] has let his imagination run away with him."

The canalists struck back. Flammarion conducted an experiment similar to Maunder's, using French schoolboys, none of whom interpreted the random marks on the paper as canals or straight lines. The canalists also claimed that the lines drawn by Lowell on his maps of Mercury and Venus differed from the Martian canals. Meanwhile, Lowell turned Antoniadi's "seeing" argument inside out. What Antoniadi called "poor seeing" (the times when the canals appeared) was actually good seeing, and what Antoniadi believed to be "excellent seeing" (the times when the canals turned into "a maze" of detail) was actually poor seeing.

Percival Lowell was too gentle a man to attack his critics, but others did so for him in a war of words. Lowell's friend Professor Edward S. Morse visited Lowell Observatory, saw the canals, and then published a book titled *Mars and Its Mystery* in 1906. A famous zoologist as well as past president of the National Academy of Sciences, Morse passionately defended his friend in his book, while condemning the views of Lowell's opponents as "balderdash" and "nonsense."

The camera provided what the canalists hoped would be the ultimate "proof" of their theories. Carl Otto Lampland came to Mars Hill to assist Lowell in 1902 and tried to photograph the canals. At the opposition in the spring of 1905, Lampland took 700 photographs of the Red Planet, some of which, claimed Lowell and his staff, showed canals.

PHOTOS PROVE LIFE ON MARS HIGHLY CIVILIZED, proclaimed newspaper headlines, and in his 1906 book, *Mars and Its Canals,* Lowell triumphantly wrote about the pictures: "There were the old configurations of patches, the light areas and the dark, just as they looked through the telescope . . . and there more marvelous yet were . . . those lines that had so piqued human curiosity, the canals of Mars."

Percival Lowell hoped that the photographs would end the controversy, but they didn't. Experts disagreed as to whether the pictures revealed canals, and when several magazines reproduced the pictures, so much clarity was lost in the publishing process that virtually no hints of canals appeared on the printed pages.

While the canal controversy continued, Lowell shifted gears. The eighth planet, Neptune, had been discovered in 1846. By the early 1900s, many astronomers felt that a ninth planet, located in a remote

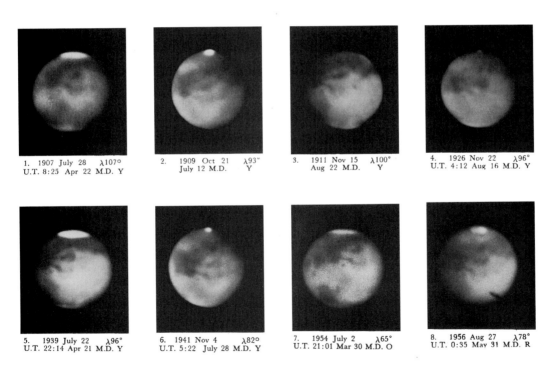

1. 1907 July 28 λ107°
U.T. 8:25 Apr 22 M.D. Y

2. 1909 Oct 21 λ93°
July 12 M.D. Y

3. 1911 Nov 15 λ100°
Aug 22 M.D. Y

4. 1926 Nov 22 λ96°
U.T. 4:12 Aug 16 M.D. Y

5. 1939 July 22 λ96°
U.T. 22:14 Apr 21 M.D. Y

6. 1941 Nov 4 λ82°
U.T. 5:22 July 28 M.D. Y

7. 1954 July 2 λ65°
U.T. 21:01 Mar 30 M.D. O

8. 1956 Aug 27 λ78°
U.T. 0:35 May 31 M.D. R

Lowell Observatory took these eight photographs of Mars between 1907 and 1956.

region of the Solar System, was pulling Uranus and Neptune out of position. In 1905, Percival Lowell began a search for this object, which he called "Planet X." Examining the entire sky for Planet X could take decades, so Lowell figured likely places to look based on the other planets' orbits. This project required so much complex mathematics that it finally earned him what he craved: the respect of other astronomers. Dr. Carl Lampland revealed that Lowell's purpose in searching for the ninth planet was to "gain more respectability for his theories about Mars."

As he and his assistants searched for Planet X, Lowell became so involved in the project that it began to rival his interest in Mars. He never saw the outcome of the Mars controversy or his planet hunt. During his last years, he worked at a frantic pace—spending nights at the telescope, writing, and lecturing. In September and October of 1916, he lectured about Mars and other topics at colleges in Washington, Idaho, Oregon, and California. Following a night at the telescope, Lowell suffered a massive stroke on November 12, 1916, and died at his observatory. He was buried at Mars Hill, near the 24-inch telescope with which he had viewed the Red Planet.

On February 18, 1930, Lowell Observatory astronomer Clyde W. Tombaugh completed Percival Lowell's Planet X project by discovering the ninth planet, which was named Pluto. Tombaugh's discovery bestowed glory on Percival Lowell's memory and upon his observatory.

But the canal controversy would not end for another thirty-five years, while the debate about life on Mars would continue long after that—and in fact is still taking place today.

Opposite page: Percival Lowell in his later years

five

The Mania for Martians

♂ **At one point** in the 1968 film *Mars Needs Women,* Dop the Martian takes the Earthwoman, Dr. Marjorie Bolen, to a planetarium show about the Red Planet. As Dop and Dr. Bolen leave the lecture, an elderly watchman remarks to them: "You know, folks really want to believe that the Martians are coming. They're bored. They want some excitement. And, after all, they come here because this is the closest thing that they can get to actually being on the planet Mars."

His comment summarizes the public's view of the canal controversy. Most people weren't interested in the dispute between astronomers and "wanted to believe in Martians" because they "wanted some excitement." The result was a flood of stories and movies about Martians, as well as new schemes for contacting the Red Planet.

The many readers of Percival Lowell's book *Mars* included Herbert George Wells, an English science-fiction author who had written *The Time Machine* and *The Invisible Man.* H. G. Wells, as he is known, recognized the seeds of a novel in Lowell's theory about giant Martians

Martian as portrayed in Thomas Edison's 1910 film, *A Trip to Mars*

living on a dry, dying world. Stories need conflict, however, so Wells discarded Lowell's conclusion that the Martians were peaceful beings who had outgrown war. Instead, he made them hostile creatures who decide to conquer Earth. The result was *The War of the Worlds* (first published as a magazine serial in 1897 and then as a novel in 1898). A century later, it is still the most famous story ever written about Mars.

"No one would have believed, in the last years of the nineteenth century, that human affairs were being watched keenly and closely by intelligences greater than man's," Wells's novel begins. "Yet, across the gulf of space, minds that are to our minds as ours are to those of the beasts, intellects vast and cool and unsympathetic, regarded this Earth with envious eyes, and slowly and surely drew their plans against us."

The first ominous signs occur when astronomers observe "outbreaks of incandescent gas" and "reddish flashes and projections" along the edge of Mars as the planet approaches opposition. These prove to be the launch of rocket ships toward Earth. The spacecraft land in England, and out of them emerge the Martian Fighting-Machines—mechanical monstrosities a hundred feet high. Within the machines are the Martians themselves—giant heads with tentacles. Attacking with their Heat-Rays and poisonous Black Smoke, the Martians easily conquer England. They don't burn up or poison everyone, though. They eat some people—taking "the fresh living blood and injecting it into their own veins."

The conquest of England appears to be "the beginning of the rout of civilization, of the massacre of mankind," the narrator reports. But then a miracle occurs. Ages earlier, Martian scientists had eliminated germs from their planet. With no resistance to Earth germs, the Martians are "slain by the bacteria against which their systems were unprepared, slain, after all man's devices had failed, by the humblest things that God, in His wisdom, has put upon the Earth." The novel closes with the Martians invading Venus and with the warning that other extraterrestrials may visit us, bringing "good or evil suddenly out of space."

Besides being a spellbinding story, *The War of the Worlds* provided food for thought. At the time, England and other powerful European nations ruled many weaker lands. Wells shows the unjustness of this by putting his readers in the place of the conquered people. Also, the conquest of Earthlings by Martians, and Martians by bacteria, is a reminder that we should not assume that we occupy the supreme place in the Universe. Ever since the appearance of *The War of the Worlds*, stories about Mars have often offered similar philosophical "messages" that apply to life on Earth.

Let us now jump forward forty years—perhaps making our journey in H. G. Wells's time machine—to October 30, 1938. At eight o'clock eastern standard time on that night before Halloween, American listeners could tune into any of ninety-two radio stations around the United States and hear an announcer say: "The Columbia Broadcasting System and its affiliated stations present *Orson Welles and the Mercury Theatre on the Air* in *War of the Worlds* by H. G. Wells. Ladies and gentlemen: the director and star of these broadcasts, Orson Welles."

The twenty-three-year-old actor and director Orson Welles (no relation to H. G. Wells) begins the story by saying: "We know now that in the early years of the twentieth century this world was being watched closely by intelligences greater than man's." For the next hour, actors perform a dramatization of the famous Martian-invasion novel. Welles moved the story from England in 1901 to New Jersey in 1939 and added many realistic touches. Numerous real towns are mentioned, and actors impersonate reporters and officials, creating a "you are there" atmosphere.

As the action begins, an announcer reads a bulletin reporting "several explosions of incandescent gas, occurring at regular intervals on the planet Mars." A short time later, a Martian spaceship crashes on a farm in Grovers Mill, New Jersey. Dispatched to the scene, reporter Carl Phillips describes what emerges from the spacecraft:

> *Ladies and gentlemen, this is the most terrifying thing I have ever witnessed. Wait a minute! Someone's crawling out of the hollow top. Someone or something. I can see peering out of that black hole two luminous disks. Are they eyes? It might be a face. Good heavens, something's wriggling out of the shadow like a gray snake. Now it's another*

one, and another. They look like tentacles to me. There, I can see the thing's body. It's large as a bear and it glistens like wet leather. But that face. It—it's indescribable. I can hardly force myself to keep looking at it. The eyes are black and gleam like a serpent. The mouth is V-shaped with saliva dripping from its rimless lips that seem to quiver and pulsate.

Reporter Phillips is still talking when the Martians activate their Heat-Ray. "The whole field's caught fire!" he says. "The woods, the barns, the gas tanks of automobiles! It's spreading everywhere. It's coming *this way,* about twenty yards to my right—" Then there is silence, for as another announcer soon reports: "The charred body of Carl Phillips has been identified in a Trenton hospital."

Soldiers are sent in to fight the Martians, but 7,000 of them die in the hopeless effort. Meanwhile, reports pour in that more Martian spaceships are landing across the country in such cities as Buffalo, Chicago, and St. Louis. Just when it seems certain that the Martians' Heat-Rays and poisonous Black Smoke will wipe out humanity, bacteria come to the rescue and destroy the enemy.

By the time the hour-long broadcast was over and the Martians had died, much of the United States was in a frenzy unique in the history of broadcasting. Despite four announcements during the broadcast that it was a fictional story, many of the eight million listeners had tuned in during the middle of the program and assumed that the Martians had really landed. Nearly two million people panicked, running off to warn neighbors and friends, phoning loved ones to say good-bye, and speeding away by automobile in the hope of escaping the invaders. Hospitals admitted a number of people for shock and hysteria. In Pittsburgh, Pennsylvania, a husband returned home just in time to prevent his wife from drinking poison. She had preferred to kill herself rather than be killed by the Martians.

Learning of the nationwide panic, the network made three more announcements following the show:

> *For those listeners who tuned in to* Orson Welles's Mercury Theatre on the Air *broadcast from eight o'clock to nine o'clock eastern standard time tonight and did not realize that the program was merely a modernized adaptation of H. G. Wells's famous novel* War of the Worlds, *we are repeating the fact which was made clear four times on the program, that, while the names of some American cities were used, as in all novels and dramatizations, the entire story and all of its incidents were fictitious.*

By the time the panic subsided on Halloween morning, many people had driven far out into the country to escape the Martians. Books were written about this famous example of "mass hysteria," including *The Invasion from Mars: A Study in the Psychology of Panic,* by Princeton University psychology professor Hadley Cantril.

Percival Lowell might have smiled at the reasons offered to explain what had happened. The leading theory was that Americans were in a panicky mood because of unsettled world conditions that would soon lead to World War II. Although this was certainly a factor, another reason was just as important. The story was about invaders from Mars. Had it been about creatures from the Moon or Saturn, who would have mistaken fiction for fact? Most people in 1938 still believed in Martians and were terrified but not surprised when they heard about the "Martian invasion."

In 1897, the year *The War of the Worlds* first appeared in print, *Auf Zwei Planeten (On Two Planets)* was published in Germany. The novel's author, Kurd Lasswitz, was a German mathematics teacher who had fallen under Percival Lowell's spell, as shown by the following passage:

> *The Martians had built a network of broad, straight canals across their deserts, and in this manner they distributed, across the entire planet when the snows melted at the beginning of the summer in each hemisphere, the water that had accumulated in the form of snow at the poles. On both shores of the canals, vegetation was plentiful. The canal network crossing the deserts created an extremely fertile belt of vegetation, about a hundred kilometers [62 miles] wide, which contained an uninterrupted chain of thriving settlements.*

Lasswitz's Martians, who resemble Earthlings physically, establish bases at our North and South Poles. Possessing an older, wiser civilization, they wish to teach us the ways of peace, asking only that we supply air and energy for their aging world. All goes smoothly when Earthlings and Martians first meet. Saltner, a German polar explorer, falls in love with La, a Martian woman. The Martians, who have developed synthetic foods, enabling them to feed a population twice that of Earth's, are willing to share their technology with us. But the spirit of friendship is suddenly destroyed when the English start fighting the interplanetary visitors and are quickly defeated.

Deciding that Earthlings are too warlike to rule themselves, the Martians conquer our planet, forsaking their peaceful ways and becoming tyrants. But scientists in the United States secretly build airships, which overwhelm the Martians in a surprise attack. The two planets make peace, with equal rights for all, and Earth appears to be on its way, as the title of the last chapter attests, to "World Peace."

The novel was enormously successful in Europe and was soon translated into Danish, Dutch, Spanish, Italian, Czech, Polish, Hungarian, Swedish, and Norwegian. The German-born rocket scientist Wernher von Braun, who later helped the United States land the first astronauts on the Moon, said that *Auf Zwei Planeten* helped spark his interest in space travel. However, the book was not translated into English until 1971, seventy-four years after it first appeared. Although packed with ideas, the novel didn't have enough action for American tastes, and readers in England weren't interested in a story in which they were the villains.

No one ever criticized an Edgar Rice Burroughs novel for lacking action. Born in 1875 in Chicago, Illinois, Burroughs daydreamed about adventures in far-off places while drifting from job to job. He served in the Army; worked as a miner, a cowboy, and a detective; ran a stationery store; and was employed by a pencil-sharpener company. Finally, he became an author and turned his daydreams into stories. Burroughs is best known for his *Tarzan* books about an English boy who is lost in the jungle and raised by apes. He also wrote novels about the Red Planet, starting with *The Princess of Mars* in 1912. Burroughs' hero, John Carter, travels to Mars in an unusual way. While out on the Arizona desert, he looks up, sees the Red Planet, then closes his eyes and wishes himself there. Carter goes from one thrilling adventure to another as he fights headless creatures, man-eating trees, and a 130-foot giant while finding time to romance the beautiful Martian princess, Dejah Thoris.

Throughout the 1900s, thousands of other science-fiction novels and stories were written about Mars. A few are fine literature, such as *The Martian Chronicles,* Ray Bradbury's 1950 classic about the end of an old Martian civilization and the colonization of the planet by Earthlings. Most are simple adventures—just the kind of tales that are perfect for movies.

The most famous inventor in history helped create one of the first "Martian movies." Thomas Edison invented the electric light and the phonograph, and helped develop motion pictures. In 1910, Edison produced *A Trip to Mars,* the story of a scientist who discovers antigravity powders that he accidentally spills on himself, launching him to the

Red Planet. Upon landing, he finds himself in a forest of gigantic tree creatures. The Martian tree monsters reach out their arms to catch him, and one nearly swallows him, but the scientist survives this nightmarish encounter and returns to Earth in a giant snowball.

A century ago, magazine serials were popular. Stories were told in installments, with pauses at exciting moments so that readers would buy the next issue of the magazine. Lowell's book *Mars* and H. G. Wells's *The War of the Worlds* originated as serials. Movies took serials to new heights of popularity. Each week, audiences packed movie theaters to see an ongoing adventure story. The action was always cut off at an exciting part—such as the hero plunging off a cliff or about to get hit by an onrushing train. All week, moviegoers debated whether the hero would survive. The next Saturday when they returned to the theater, they were relieved to find the hero still alive, although within minutes he was sure to land in a new "pickle."

Scene from the 1938 serial *Mars Attacks the World*. Dr. Zarkov is at left. Flash Gordon has the lightning streak across his chest.

The movie serial *Mars Attacks the World* was released in 1938—the year of *The War of the Worlds* radio broadcast—but except for the Martian connection and similar titles, the two stories had little in common. Based on the "Flash Gordon" comic strip, *Mars Attacks the World* is a fast-paced adventure that couldn't be mistaken for reality.

As the story begins, a mysterious ray from space is causing hurricanes and other disasters on Earth. Suspecting that the evil Emperor Ming the Merciless is to blame, the daring Earthman Flash Gordon, his lady love Dale Arden, and their scientist friend Dr. Zarkov blast off in their rocket toward Ming's planet, Mongo. On the way, Zarkov discovers: "That beam of light is coming from Mars! We're being pulled straight to Mars!"

Once on Mars, Flash and his companions learn that the Red Planet's Queen Azura and her ally Ming are using a "Nitron Lamp" to suck away Earth's atmosphere. But Azura is foolish to trust Ming, whose true goal is to conquer *both* Earth and Mars. Ming kills Azura, and after a series of clashes with the Earth people, he announces: "I want to destroy Earth! The Earth can not survive! It is written that all of the planets shall be destroyed but one [Ming's planet, Mongo]. And the Earth shall be first!" But just as Ming aims his Nitron Lamp toward Earth at full power, Flash Gordon comes to the rescue along with one of the evil emperor's own assistants who realizes that he has gone mad. After thwarting Ming's evil plans, Flash and his friends return to Earth as heroes. Viewing the *Mars Attacks the World* serial for the first time in forty years a short while ago, I noticed that, in a kind of side plot, Flash is assisted on Mars by the Clay People, who live underground. Today's scientists think that Mars may actually *have* underground life—but only simple microbes rather than Clay People.

A few years after *Mars Attacks the World* appeared, the flying saucer furor began. Although unidentified flying objects (UFOs) had been seen earlier, the phenomenon was rarely reported until 1947. On June 24, businessman and deputy sheriff Kenneth Arnold was flying his airplane over Washington State when he noticed nine disk-shaped objects traveling at what he estimated to be nearly 2,000 miles per hour—faster than any aircraft of the time. Arnold reported that the objects flew like saucers (dishes that hold cups), and so they became known as "flying saucers." Ever since, flying saucers or UFOs have been regularly reported around the world.

By the 1950s, many people believed that flying saucers were alien spacecraft. Observers began to report seeing UFOs up close—blocking roads and hovering over fields and houses. Some people have claimed to have been taken aboard UFOs by extraterrestrials. What lies behind these reports? As with the earlier canal controversy, there are sharp differences of opinion. Most scientists think that UFOs are misidentifications of ordinary objects such as helicopters and weather balloons, and that people who say they have boarded alien spacecraft are overly imaginative. Yet, among the public, the belief is widespread that UFOs are visitors from space.

Periods of especially numerous sightings are called *flying saucer*

Photo of a UFO, taken through a car window

waves. In the 1950s, it was noted that the waves tended to occur when Mars was at opposition. Again, there were disagreements as to why. The Martians visit Earth when their planet is relatively nearby, said the believers in flying saucers. People slip into a "flying saucer mood" when Mars is unusually bright, countered the scoffers.

The flying saucer craze of the 1950s and 1960s inspired dozens of Martian movies, including the 1953 classic, *Invaders from Mars.* The hero of this film, a boy named David, is an amateur astronomer who sees a flying saucer land near his home. The craft contains Martians, who are so intelligent that they are just bodiless heads and who have come to Earth to prevent the launching of spacecraft that might destroy their civilization. With the help of their big, green, robotlike servants, the Martians take control of the townspeople, including David's parents, by implanting devices in their necks. David seeks help from an astronomer friend, Dr. Stuart Kelston, with whom he has a Lowellian conversation:

> **Professor Kelston:** *We're not very much in the overall scheme of things. Life can and does exist on other planets. But if we have invaders from outer space, they probably came from one of the nearer planets.*
> **David:** *Mars?*
> **Kelston:** *Some form of life exists on Mars. You see, Mars is an old and perhaps dying world.*
> **David:** *There's oxygen in its atmosphere, and water vapor. There was life on Mars a long, long time before there was ever life on Earth.*
> **Kelston:** *There is a theory that their cities are underground or that they live in spaceships.*

With Dr. Kelston's help, David leads an Army attack on the aliens. A surprise ending helped *Invaders from Mars* become so successful that the film was remade during the 1980s.

The movie version of *The War of the Worlds* was also released in 1953. Although they moved the story's setting to California in the 1950s, the moviemakers retained the novel's frightening elements and added a few of their own. For example, the movie came out during the Cold War, a period when there was tremendous fear of a nuclear war. In one scene, the United States drops atomic bombs on the Martian space-craft without making a dent. Atomic bombs had not existed in H. G. Wells's time, but the scene supports his theme that we may not be as powerful as we think.

Camille Flammarion's favorite Martian movie might have been *The Angry Red Planet*. The four astronauts in this 1960 thriller land on Mars and are attacked by red monsters. The astronauts encounter a 40-foot-tall bat-rat-spider, a gigantic human-eating plant, a sea monster, and Martians with three bulging eyes. The Martians drive the astronauts away because humans are too warlike, as they explain in a recorded message sent back to Earth:

> *We of the planet Mars give you this warning. For centuries we have watched you, listened to your radio signals, and learned your speech. And now you have invaded our home. Your civilization has not progressed beyond destruction, war, and violence. Do as you will to your own, but remember this warning: DO NOT RETURN TO MARS! WE CAN AND WILL DESTROY YOU—ALL LIFE ON YOUR PLANET, IF YOU DO NOT HEED US. Go now, warn mankind not to return unbidden.*

Perhaps the weirdest Martian movie begins with Earth scientists decoding a radio signal from the Red Planet that provides the film's title: *Mars Needs Women*. This chilling warning proves true, for, with

Opposite Page: Bodiless Martian as seen in the 1953 classic film *Invaders from Mars*

The Martians arrived in flying saucers in the 1953 film version of
The War of the Worlds.

their civilization threatened by a shortage of females, five Martians come to kidnap five Earthwomen and take them to their planet. The aliens' plan succeeds until one of them, Dop, falls in love with an intended victim, space scientist Dr. Marjorie Bolen. In this 1968 feature's best scene, Dop and Dr. Bolen go to a planetarium show about Mars. When the tape-recorded lecture breaks down, Dop takes over and tells the audience:

> *Mars, the one planet that shows evidence of being habitable. Mars has polar caps over the North and South Poles. Between those polar caps is one of the biggest controversies about Mars, the crisscrossing of a network of canals. Many believe that these canals are part of a vast irrigation system, by which water is pumped from the polar caps to supply the needs of the rest of the planet. Yes, the conditions for life do exist on Mars. But unless it can renew itself, the first Earth explorers will find only the sad remnants of a civilization that was brighter than that of the Earth but that may turn to dust.*

At that moment, Dr. Bolen realizes that Dop is a Martian, but she doesn't care. She loves him. At the climax of *Mars Needs Women*, Dop must decide whether to return to Mars with his companions or remain on Earth with the woman he loves.

Bizarre though they were, the movies and stories about Mars were matched by equally strange real-life events. Percival Lowell's writings and lectures inspired new plans for contacting Mars. In the 1890s, it was suggested that the Great Pyramid near Cairo, Egypt, be illuminated with bright lights that the Martians might see through their telescopes. A few years later, a self-proclaimed psychic named Sackville Leyson tried to transmit his spirit to Mars while his body remained at home in Syracuse, New York. In 1906, Leyson claimed to have succeeded, traveling to Mars and back in 40 minutes. He reported that "two tribes of people" live on Mars. "The larger species have huge ears, a nose like a lion, and only one eye in the middle of the forehead. The little men live in holes in the ground. They have two eyes and no nose, but there is a hole in each cheek."

As the most favorable opposition of September 1909 approached, there was an outbreak of "Mars fever." On April 25, the *New York Times* devoted a full page to an article titled PICKERING'S IDEA FOR SIGNALING MARS. William H. Pickering prefaced his remarks by explaining: "I would not deny the existence of intelligent life on Mars, but I think it has not been proved. My idea to settle the matter is to send messages. If return signals come to the Earth in answer, they would prove that there are intelligent beings on Mars. If not, the existence of such beings on that planet would be, to my mind, doubtful."

Pickering then described his plan: "Fix 50 mirrors, each 25 feet square, on a shaft like the axis of a telescope. There should be 50 shafts, bringing the total number of mirrors up to 2,500. This would make a quarter of a mile square of mirrors. By this means a steady flash of light bright enough to be visible through a telescope would be sent from the Earth to Mars." If they detected the flashes, the Martians would probably "erect some apparatus" to return the signals, continued Pickering. "Then, as soon as flashes similar to those sent from the Earth were answered from Mars, a system of dots and dashes like those used in the telegraphic code could be employed. If these were answered with like dots and dashes, it would settle beyond doubt the existence of intelligent beings on Mars."

No one stepped forward with the $10 million needed to finance Pickering's project. A junior version of this plan was to assemble many thousands of people on the Texas plains, where they would hold mirrors and flash sunlight at Mars. The problem was finding volunteers willing to do this.

Also in 1909, Johns Hopkins University physicist R. W. Wood proposed that an array of motor-driven revolving cylinders, covered on one side by a huge round black cloth, be set up in a desert. As the motors turned the cylinders, the black cloth would face the sky at times but disappear when on the side facing the ground, much the way an escalator works. Viewing Earth, Martian astronomers would see a black dot alternately appear and disappear. No one offered to sew a cloth almost as big as a state or to build the complex machinery needed to drive the signaling device.

There were other ideas in the early 1900s. Huge assemblies of electric lights could be switched on and off in synchronized patterns to signal Mars. Words could be written in gigantic letters on the desert. A 32,000-square-mile flag (roughly the size of the state of Maine) could be constructed. As with the other schemes, none of these grandiose projects was attempted.

Most people considered it easier to locate signals from the Red Planet than to send messages there. In 1895, a scientist in Washington, D.C., was studying a map of the Martian canals that accompanied a Percival Lowell paper when he noticed something remarkable. Several canal configurations resembled Hebrew letters that spelled a name for God. Surely the Martians were attempting to communicate with us in one of our oldest languages, he concluded. NAME OF GOD ON MARS, announced the *New York Herald* on May 19, 1895. "True," the newspaper admitted, "the magnitude of the work of cutting the canals into the shape of the name of God is at first thought appalling." But then the article pointed out that the task was less difficult than it seemed, because the Martians were far stronger than ourselves. Although the scientist who made this "discovery" wished to remain anonymous, the *Herald* assured its readers that "there can be no doubt of the observer's accuracy."

Five years later, the Martians seemed to be at it again. On December 7 and 8 of the year 1900, Lowell Observatory's Andrew E. Douglass observed a "white projection" on the edge of Mars. He thought it was an interesting natural phenomenon, but it was widely reported as a message from the Martians. French newspapers proclaimed SIGNAUX SUR MARS (SIGNALS ON MARS) and LES SIGNAUX DE LA PLANETE MARS (THE SIGNALS FROM THE PLANET MARS). Recalling that the recently published *War of the Worlds*

Years ago, Martian costumes were popular among children on Halloween and among adults attending costume parties.

began with similar "projections," some people feared that the Martians were about to attack.

When he resumed work in 1901 following his nervous breakdown, Percival Lowell explained that the "projection" was probably a large cloud hanging over a Martian swamp. When Lowell himself saw a "projection" along the edge of Mars on May 26, 1903, he explained it away as "an enormous cloud," but headlines announced MESSAGES FROM MARS once again. That August, the *London Daily Mail* ran an article titled SIGNALS FROM THE STARS, which began:

Is Mars inhabited by intelligent beings who are trying to signal us? This question is again brought to the front by the announcement that Professor Lowell—who of all living astronomers knows most about the red planet—has just observed a brilliant projection from the edge of its disk. The brilliant imaginations of H. G. Wells have familiarized us all with the possibilities of life on Mars and no one who has read The War of the Worlds *can help shuddering slightly when he remembers that just such a projection indicated the commencement of that terrifying invasion.*

Mars generated more excitement in 1904, when what was apparently a giant dust storm on the planet produced a W-shaped formation. Because images in astronomical telescopes appear upside down, the shape could also be viewed as an M. A similar M- or W-shaped formation was spotted on Mars in 1954. In both cases, people debated whether it stood for *Martians* or *war*.

Guglielmo Marconi invented the radio in 1895. We now know that phenomena such as lightning, magnetic storms on the Sun, and electrical machinery can cause static and other interference with radio broadcasts. But in radio's pioneer days, such disturbances were often thought to be messages from Mars. Nikola Tesla, inventor of the AC (alternating current) motor, which is used in many household appliances, became convinced that he was intercepting Martian radio signals. Born in what became Yugoslavia, Tesla later moved to the United States and set up a radio laboratory in Colorado Springs, Colorado. One night in 1899, Tesla detected electrical disturbances of unknown origin. "The feeling is constantly growing in me that I had been the first to hear the greeting of one planet to another," he said. "According to my investigations, [the signals] could not have originated from the Sun, the Moon, or Venus," he determined. "Further study has satisfied me that they must have emanated from Mars."

The possibility of messages from Mars also intrigued the inventor of radio. Around 1920, Guglielmo Marconi believed that he had detected broadcasts from the Red Planet. However, these "broadcasts" were probably "whistlers"—radio signals caused by discharges of distant lightning. As for Tesla, radio experts are certain that whatever he heard were not broadcasts from Mars.

Astronomer David Todd of Amherst College in Massachusetts hoped to make radio contact with Mars. As the 1909 opposition approached, Todd planned to ascend in a balloon with a radio and listen for Martian broadcasts. "If life really exists on Mars," Todd explained, "they have been trying for years to get into conversation with us, and perhaps wonder what manner of stupid things we are not to respond. We might [intercept their radio signals] if we could get high enough, away from the noises and other waves that surround us, up in the rarefied regions of our atmosphere with nothing to disturb the communication."

Sounding like the somewhat pretentious title character in L. Frank Baum's novel *Wonderful Wizard of Oz,* published nine years earlier, Todd continued: "In mounting high up in the balloon to attempt to intercept any ether [radio] waves, I shall be shut into a metal box made of aluminum for lightness and fitted with apparatus to drive out the carbonic acid gas and supply oxygen and with air pressure to prevent sickness. In that way I can ascend much higher than balloons have heretofore gone." While searching for radio messages from Mars, he added, he would also listen for signals from "Venus or any other of the planets."

Todd never got off the ground in 1909, but he kept trying. In 1912, he climbed to the top of one of the Andes Mountains in South America, where he attempted to establish contact with Mars. In 1913, he actually did ascend in a balloon but failed to achieve the great height he wanted and landed in Canada without communicating with extraterrestrials. On August 23, 1924, Mars made its closest approach to Earth of the twentieth century. Todd proposed that every radio station on Earth close down to clear the airways for Martian broadcasts. Although most stations refused, several commercial stations and numerous U.S. Navy and Army stations went silent so that experts could listen for signals from Mars. William F. Friedman, head of the code department for the Army Signal Corps, stood ready to translate any Martian messages.

During that 1924 opposition, a radio expert in Vancouver, Canada, claimed that he detected signals that "cannot be attributed to any known instrument." They proved to be radio transmissions from the United States. Unusual radio signals were also reported in England, but they, too, were of non-Martian origin. Another false alarm occurred when radiophoto equipment (apparatus for converting radio waves into pictures) in Washington, D.C., produced an image that happened to resemble a "crudely drawn face." Of course, some people assumed the so-called face was a self-portrait transmitted by a Martian.

The November 4, 1926, opposition marked the last major outbreak of "Mars fever." In the days before the Red Planet's close approach,

If Martians attacked the Russians, whose side would we be on?

There's only one answer:

We're all on this thing together.

Even if we don't get along with some nations, we've got to deal with the great problems that affect all nations: not Martians but pollution, population, trade barriers, restricted freedoms to travel, war.

They're just too big and too urgent for even the strongest nations to solve alone.

One way to develop solutions is by getting together with nations we *are* friendly with... some of our European allies and other autonomous democracies.

In the next session of Congress, a resolution will be introduced calling for a convention of delegates from the most experienced democracies.

This Atlantic Union Convention will explore the possibilities of forming a workable federation of democracies, geared to finding and implementing practical solutions to our mutual troubles.

By utilizing the individual strengths and talents of each free nation, we can begin to set things straight on the only world we've got.

We can pull the peoples of the world together by solving the difficulties we face together.

The concept of a federation of autonomous democracies is not new. Beginning in 1939 with Clarence K. Streit's non-fiction best-seller, *Union Now*, it has won the support of such diverse leaders as Robert Kennedy, Barry Goldwater, Hubert Humphrey, Richard Nixon and George McGovern among others.

President Kennedy described it this way:

"Acting on our own by ourselves, we cannot establish justice throughout the world. We cannot insure its domestic tranquility, or provide for its common defense or promote its general welfare, or secure the blessings of liberty to ourselves and our posterity. But, joined with other free nations, we can do all of this and more..."

Unfortunately there are people in this country who are against our simply participating in the Atlantic Union discussions.

So we need your support.

By filling out and mailing this coupon, you'll simply be saying "Why not? Let's talk."

My planet, right or wrong.

☐ I'm interested in knowing more about the history and concept of federal union. Please send me more information.

☐ I'm interested in joining TOGETHER, to help unite all peoples against our common problems. Enclosed is $5.00 which entitles me to your newsletter and educational materials.

together
1736 Columbia Rd. N.W.
Washington, D.C. 20009
Suite 401

Name _____

Address _____

City _____ State _____ Zip _____

This ad is sponsored by Youth for Federal Union, a private, non-profit, educational organization dedicated to the development of intelligent support for the creation of a federal union of democratic nations.

Martians have often been mentioned in advertisements because they catch people's attention. This poster was issued to promote world peace.

people switched their radio dials back and forth, hoping to locate a Martian broadcast. An Englishman, Dr. Mansfield Robinson, insisted that messages were being transmitted through space from Martians' brains directly to his own. He claimed he had learned from these telepathic messages that "Martians are intelligent, stand eight feet tall, have large ears, and long hair. Another, lower kind of Martian has the head of a walrus." Dr. Robinson went to London's Central Telegraph Office and asked to send a telegram. When the telegraph operator asked its destination, Dr. Robinson responded, "Mars." The telegraph office charged Robinson 18 pence (36 cents) a word, the long-distance rate, but there was no reply from Mars.

English astronomer Edward Walter Maunder had a simple explanation about our failure to communicate with Mars. Along with a growing number of astronomers, Maunder believed that Mars was uninhabited (although he thought that Venus might very well be home to extraterrestrials). Ever the optimist, Camille Flammarion offered a different explanation for the Martians' silence. After the 1924 opposition yielded no tangible results, the eighty-two-year-old Flammarion told reporters at his observatory near Paris: "Perhaps the Martians tried before, in the time of the dinosaur, to contact Earth, and got tired when no one responded."

Pioneer aviator Claude Collins offered to settle the dispute about Mars. If a rocket could be built to transport him there safely, he would fly to the Red Planet and see whether it was inhabited. Collins didn't have to worry about anyone accepting his challenge. Not until a few years after Collins made his offer did a human being make a rocket flight, and that lasted only a mile—a long way from Mars.

Until far more powerful rockets were built, people would continue to theorize and argue about life on Mars. Little did they suspect that, even after spacecraft were built that *could* land on Mars, the speculation would continue.

six

First Spacecraft to Mars

♂ **By the 1920s,** what has been called the "delowellization" of Mars had begun. New giant telescopes provided improved views of Mars and other heavenly bodies. In California, a 100-inch reflector was installed at Mount Wilson Observatory in 1917, and a 200-inch reflector, still one of the world's great telescopes, began operating at Palomar Observatory in 1948. Other instruments also helped provide information about Mars. With *thermocouples*—electric devices that measure heat—astronomers learned more about the planet's climate. With *spectroscopes*—instruments that analyze light from heavenly bodies—they learned about Mars's atmosphere.

With each new discovery, the existence of Martians seemed less likely. The canals did not appear at all through the larger telescopes. Thermocouple measurements made during the 1920s indicated that Mars's average temperature was a frigid -10 degrees F—far below Earth's average of 57 degrees F. Spectrographic studies made during the 1930s revealed that the Martian atmosphere has very little oxygen or water—substances needed by human beings, plants, and animals on Earth.

Although observers with relatively small telescopes occasionally reported seeing canals, by the 1950s, the vast majority of astronomers had rejected Percival Lowell's theory about canal-building Martians. In his 1950 book *The Planet Mars,* French astronomer Gérard de Vaucouleurs called Lowell's theories "fairy tales" and dismissed the canals as "illusions created by inadequate instruments, which vanish when studied with powerful apparatus." In his 1956 book *A Space Traveler's Guide to Mars,* American astronomer I. M. Levitt wrote: "With good telescopes, the canals are not to be seen [and are] most certainly not the product of a superior intelligence inhabiting the planet." That same year, in his astronomy book *And There Was Light,* German author Rudolf Thiel called the canals "optical illusions" that "become grains or spots when viewed under the best conditions with the finest instruments."

Yet the same astronomers who scoffed at the prospect of Martians still insisted that Mars had plant life. In 1940, English astronomer H. Spencer Jones wrote in his book *Life on Other Worlds* that "there is pretty conclusive evidence of the presence of vegetation on Mars." He added that the Martian vegetation "is akin" to Earth's dry mosses, which can survive with very little water, and lichens, which grow on rocks and can survive extreme cold. Levitt thought that "vegetation appears to be the only explanation for the dark markings on Mars," while Thiel believed that Mars "at best has simple forms of plant life." Like Edward Walter Maunder, Thiel was more confident about life on Venus, which he thought might have a "dripping wet climate for moisture-loving plants and swamp animals."

Like the hardy lichens and mosses of the Arctic, though, Percival Lowell's views survived among the public. In fact, thanks in part to all the science-fiction movies and novels about Mars, the new information barely dented the popular view about Martians. As an amateur astronomer growing up in the 1950s, I was often asked by friends and relatives gazing through my telescope, "Are there really Martians?" and "Can we see the canals?" These questions were asked so often that I prepared a minilecture, explaining that while we astronomers were 99 percent certain that Mars had no intelligent life, we believed its greenish areas were plants.

But what we say isn't necessarily what we think—or hope. On July 30, 1960, my fourteen-year-old self wrote in an "Observing Notebook": "Around 1:45 in the morning, I began observation of the red planet, which was coming up in Taurus, in the east. I am positive of seeing some smallish detail on the disk." A few months later, on November 10, I drew a picture of Mars that shows the Syrtis Major. However, my sketch makes this Y-shaped dark area look like three canals. Was I trying to convince myself that I had seen the canals of Mars?

Not long afterward, Mars figured in one of my most terrifying experiences. On December 30, 1960, Mars reached opposition. On a sub-zero night around that time, I observed Mars for several hours and was so hypnotized by the Red Planet that I didn't notice my legs becoming

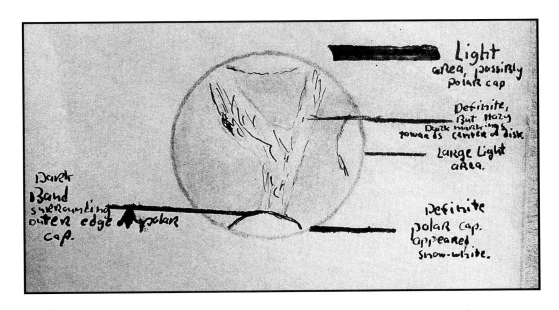

The author made this sketch of Mars as seen through his telescope on November 10, 1960, when he was fourteen years old.

numb. When I tried to walk inside, I fell to the ground and had to drag myself upstairs to pour warm water on my legs. After about a half hour, feeling in my legs returned, but ever since, I have had minor leg problems—a reminder of the night forty years ago when I fell under Mars's spell and forgot to come in out of the cold.

A few professional astronomers of the 1950s continued to believe in the canals. Earl C. Slipher, who obtained more than 100,000 photographs of Mars during his nearly sixty years with Lowell Observatory, insisted on the canals' "existence as true markings on the planet" until his death at age eighty-one in 1964. For a time, NASA (the National Aeronautics and Space Administration, created in 1958) used Slipher's canal-covered models as its maps of Mars.

The Space Age began on October 4, 1957, when Russia launched *Sputnik 1,* the first human-made satellite to orbit Earth. The United States followed in 1958 with *Explorer 1,* its first Earth-orbiting satellite. In 1960, as one artificial satellite after another was going aloft, a Russian scientist proposed a strange theory about Mars's moons. Astronomers had noted oddities in the orbit of the inner moon, Phobos, since the 1940s. Astrophysicist Iosif S. Shklovskii suggested that Phobos (and perhaps Deimos) was not a natural satellite, but a hollow space station, placed in orbit by a vanished Martian civilization.

While scientists scoffed, believers in extraterrestrials and flying saucers were enchanted by the idea. Shklovskii's theory became a launching pad for all sorts of far-fetched ideas: the two little moons had eluded discovery until 1877 because the Martians hadn't created them until then; perhaps survivors of the Martian civilization still lived inside Phobos and Deimos; the satellites had been built by inhabitants of a distant planet who used them as rest stations before continuing on to Earth; the extraterrestrials sent more spaceships Earthward when Mars was relatively near us, accounting for the "flying saucer waves" around opposition time.

During the 1960s, both the United States and Russia sent robotic spacecraft called *space probes* to the Moon. Then, on July 20, 1969, the greatest achievement in space exploration thus far occurred when American astronauts Neil Armstrong and Edwin "Buzz" Aldrin became the first human beings to walk on the Moon. As the two men gathered samples and performed experiments, they saw for themselves that the Moon is a bleak, airless, and lifeless place.

The United States and Russia also began sending probes to the planets. In 1962, the U.S. *Mariner 2* passed within 22,000 miles of Venus. *Mariner 2* discovered that Venus's temperatures exceed 800 degrees F—hot enough to melt zinc, a metal used in U.S. pennies, and also hot enough to end speculation about Venus being a home for "moisture-loving plants and swamp animals." Any dinosaur or human set down on Venus without protection would be quickly broiled.

Mars proved to be far more difficult to reach than Venus. On October 10, 1960, Russia launched a probe aimed at the Red Planet. It and four more Russian probes launched over the next two years all failed, as did the United States' *Mariner 3,* sent aloft on November 5, 1964. Less than a month later, the United States tried again, launching *Mariner 4* on November 28, 1964.

About halfway to Mars, *Mariner 4* developed trouble, but it survived and continued on through space. On July 14, 1965, seven and a half months after launch, *Mariner 4* made its closest approach to Mars, coming within about 6,100 miles of the planet. The probe took twenty-two images, the first close-up pictures ever obtained of Mars.

As the photographs were transmitted to the computers at NASA's Jet Propulsion Laboratory in Pasadena, California, the world waited to learn if there was life on Mars. The pictures revealed more in a few minutes than astronomers had learned in all the previous years of studying Mars.

Mars had no evidence of canals or vegetation.

With hundreds of craters on its surface, Mars seemed to resemble our own desolate Moon.

Mars's atmosphere was much thinner than had been previously thought—only 1 percent as thick as Earth's—and could not support any advanced forms of life as we know it. If human beings were set down on Mars without space suits, they would die within minutes. Newspapers began to call the Red Planet "the Dead Planet."

Mariner 6 and *Mariner 7,* both of which passed within 2,000 miles of Mars in the summer of 1969, enhanced our picture of Mars as a forbidding world. Together, these two probes took 200 high-quality photographs of Mars. Again, there was no sign of canals or any form of life. Measurements taken by the *Mariners* indicated that, while temperatures at Mars's equator could reach a balmy 60 degrees F at noon, nighttime temperatures on the planet dipped to more than 100 degrees below zero. Polar temperatures plunged to 200 below. By comparison, Earth's all-time coldest temperature was -129 degrees F. The Red Planet's polar caps, long believed to be snow and water ice, seemed to be frozen carbon dioxide (known as dry ice and used on Earth to refrigerate medicines and foods).

The *Mariners* ended the canal controversy forever. The cobweb of canals that Percival Lowell and so many others had reported did not appear in the *Mariner* images and had been an optical illusion. Edward Walter Maunder's experiment with schoolchildren had been on target: We sometimes interpret barely visible features as straight lines, as I saw for myself recently when I conducted a similar experiment with fourth-graders at West School in Glencoe, Illinois. Viewing the sketch I had drawn of a circle filled with dots and squiggles from about 50 feet away, many of the students claimed they saw lines crossing the picture, even though there were none. Afterward, one girl offered the best explanation of the "canal illusion" I've heard: "Our eyes played the connect-the-dot game."

Despite the evidence to the contrary, a few astronomers of the 1960s and 1970s held out hope for living organisms on Mars. Their leading spokesperson was Carl Sagan, who as a child growing up in Brooklyn,

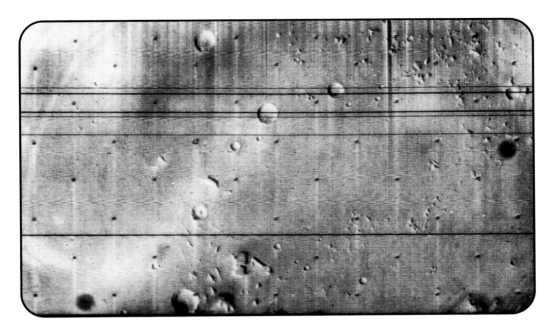

Mariner 9 took this photo of Mars in 1971.

New York, had stared at Mars from a vacant lot and tried to wish himself there like Edgar Rice Burroughs' hero John Carter. Author of astronomy books, host of the TV series *Cosmos (Cosmos* is another word for *Universe),* and Cornell University astronomy professor, Sagan was in many ways a throwback to Percival Lowell and Camille Flammarion.

Partly as a result of the misinformation and confusion caused by Lowell's canal theory, modern astronomers test their findings exhaustively and are wary of being misquoted by the media (as recently occurred when it was reported that astronomers had found *plants* instead of *planets* around a distant star). Sagan, to the contrary, loved to theorize, liberally sprinkling his speculations with the words *perhaps* and *possibly* to emphasize that he was merely brainstorming. His ideas about Mars helped to make him a bright astronomical "star" among the public but a sometimes controversial figure among his colleagues.

We don't know enough to dismiss the possibility of life on Mars yet, Sagan argued. Perhaps Mars has advanced life-forms that thrive in conditions vastly unlike those on Earth. Possibly most of Mars is hostile to life, but the planet has a few *microenvironments*—isolated, warm, wet spots—where life flourishes. Mars may be dead today, Sagan continued, but the planet may have had life long ago when its conditions were different. If so, we might find the remains of a Martian civilization. Even if Mars never had advanced life, it might have microbes (for example, bacteria or algae), possibly underground where conditions aren't as harsh as on the surface.

At first glance, searching for microbes on Mars may not seem exciting. Why should we care if Mars has organisms that can be seen only with a microscope? Carl Sagan made the prospect of finding microbes on Mars seem *very* exciting by pointing out that it could help us answer the question: Are there intelligent creatures besides ourselves in the Universe?

Our Sun, one of many trillions of stars in the Cosmos, has just one planet (Earth) known to have life. From this lone sample, we can't judge whether life, and especially intelligent life, is rare or plentiful in the Universe. But if life was found to have also developed on Mars, it would mean that organisms exist on at least two of the Sun's nine planets. That would show a trend, leading us to think that life is abundant in the Universe, and that some of it is probably intelligent. Viewed in that light, finding any form of life on Mars—even microscopic organisms—would have monumental significance.

Carl Sagan once called Mars "the planet of surprises." Every time astronomers think they understand the Red Planet, something new is discovered that prompts them to revise their theories. This was what occurred in the early 1970s when we discovered that the Red Planet might not be the Dead Planet after all.

The United States and Russia took advantage of the most favorable opposition of 1971 by launching a total of five Mars probes. The three Russian probes failed, the U.S. *Mariner 8* crashed into the ocean, but *Mariner 9* was a success, reaching Mars orbit on November 13 after a five-and-one-half-month journey.

Mariner 9 arrived during a global dust storm on Mars, prompting jokes among NASA scientists that the Martians had created the storm to hide from the cameras. While waiting for the dust to settle, the probe began photographing Mars's two little moons, putting another theory to rest. Obviously not hollow space stations, the moons are rocky, cratered, football-shaped objects. The oddities in Phobos's orbit are connected with its closeness to Mars. Gradually spiraling closer to Mars, Phobos will crash into the planet in about 50 million years.

Mariner 9 eventually transmitted more than 7,000 photographs over a period of nearly a year, enabling scientists to compile the first comprehensive map of another planet. Some of the views astounded astronomers.

Close-up views of Mars's moons, Phobos (lower right) and Deimos (lower left). At top is an asteroid named Gaspra that resembles the Martian moons.

Mariner 9 revealed that Mars has gigantic volcanic mountains, including Olympus Mons, the highest known mountain in the Solar System. Olympus Mons is approximately 350 miles across at its base and 15 miles tall—three times the height of Mount Everest, Earth's highest peak. Mars's greenish areas, such as the Syrtis Major, are neither water, as early astronomers thought, nor vegetation, as Percival Lowell believed. They are dark volcanic and rocky regions that sometimes take on a greenish hue through telescopes. The planet was also found to have a gigantic canyon, which was named Valles Marineris (Mariner Valley). Although nicknamed the "Grand Canyon of Mars," Valles Marineris dwarfs Arizona's famous canyon. With a 3,000-mile length, a 400-mile width, and a depth of up to 6 miles, Valles Marineris is ten times as long, twenty times as wide, and six times as deep as the Grand Canyon. If located in the United States, it would stretch across the country from California to New York.

But *Mariner 9*'s most mind-boggling discovery was that tremendous amounts of water once flowed across Mars. If you have ever seen a dry riverbed, you can tell from its contours that it once contained water. *Mariner 9* detected thousands of dry Martian riverbeds. These winding channels are natural features and have no connection with the canals described by Lowell and Schiaparelli, which were reported as straight and artificial-looking.

What does this discovery mean? On Earth, water is vital to life. Life may have begun in Earth's oceans, and today a remarkable variety of creatures, from microorganisms to half-million-pound blue whales, live in water habitats. Every living thing, including two-thirds of the human body, is made up mainly of water. So closely linked are water and life in our experience that it is difficult to view the dry Martian riverbeds *without* wondering if plants and animals once inhabited the planet.

The fact that Mars once had flowing water tells a larger story. The Red Planet is now so cold and dry, and its atmosphere is so thin, that

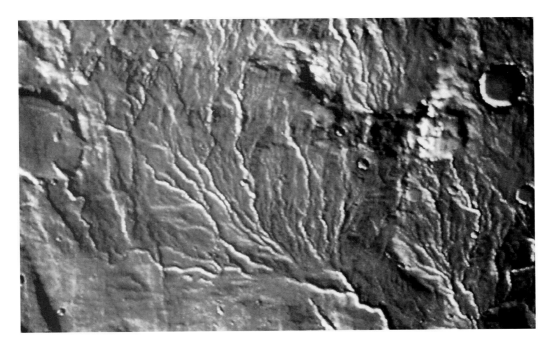

Dry riverbeds on Mars

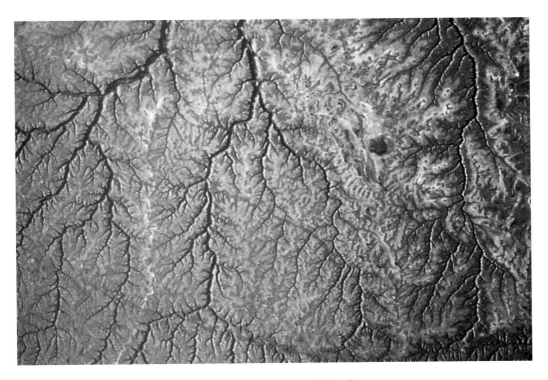

Dry riverbeds on Earth

water could not flow freely over its surface for any length of time. It would either freeze or evaporate. This leads us to think that, long ago, when Mars had flowing water, it may have had a warmer climate and a thicker atmosphere than it has today.

The discovery raised new questions. What happened to Mars's water? Why did the atmosphere thin out, and where did the gases go? Why did the planet's climate turn colder?

It is thought that the bulk of Mars's water escaped into the atmosphere, and from there into space, but that a portion of it trickled down inside Mars, where it rests in mostly frozen and partly liquid form today. Mars's gravity did not hold on to its atmospheric gases as efficiently as does our larger Earth. Some of the gases may have leaked into space or entered the soil. Regarding Mars's climate change, perhaps the Red Planet, like Earth, has ice ages. Conceivably, Mars is now in the midst of one of these prolonged cold periods and will eventually be at least somewhat warmer than it is today.

Scientists disagree about the reasons for Earth's ice ages and about other events in our planet's earlier history, so we cannot expect astronomers to agree as to why Mars has changed so dramatically over millions of years. Still, the important fact is that, long ago, Mars seems to have been more like Earth than it is currently. In those times, perhaps Mars had plants and animals, whose fossils lie buried across the planet. The Martian volcanoes seem quiet now, but volcanic areas can have *hot spots*—places where the ground temperature is higher than normal. Perhaps these hot spots provide the microenvironments Carl Sagan spoke of, where life might still exist today.

With a minimum distance of 862 miles above Mars's surface, *Mariner 9* approached very close to the planet. But to determine whether Mars has or has ever had life, it appeared that we would have to land probes—or even people—directly on the Red Planet.

seven

The Vikings Land on Mars

♂ **By the 1970s,** Earthlings were eager to see the view from the surface of Mars.

In late 1971, Russia's *Mars 2* and *Mars 3* probes both reached orbit around the Red Planet and released landers. The *Mars 2* lander became the first human-made object to arrive on Mars, but it crashed, providing no information. The *Mars 3* lander descended without mishap, but unfortunately, it arrived during the same dust storm that obscured *Mariner 9*'s view of Mars. Apparently toppled by powerful winds, the Russian craft provided no pictures or data about the Martian surface.

Meanwhile, the United States planned to land spacecraft of its own on Mars. The United States constructed twin probes, *Viking 1* and *Viking 2,* equipping each with an orbiter and a lander. The *Viking* mission was expected to reveal a world of information about Mars, with its primary goal being to determine whether life existed on the planet.

Viking 1's blastoff was scheduled for August 11, 1975. Two minutes prior to liftoff, a valve on the launch rocket malfunctioned. Launch was rescheduled for August 14, but the mission, which 10,000 people had taken eight years to assemble, could not depart then, either. A switch in the spacecraft had been left in the ON position, draining a battery.

Finally, on August 20, 1975, *Viking 1* departed for Mars. On September 9, *Viking 2* was launched. After a voyage of nearly a year, the *Vikings* entered orbit around the Red Planet.

NASA scientists hoped to set the *Viking 1* lander down on Mars on July 4, 1976—the nation's two hundredth birthday—but the intended arrival site proved to be more rugged than anticipated. Fearing that the vehicle would tip over, as had apparently befallen Russia's *Mars 3,* scientists chose a new landing site.

Early on the morning of July 20, a technician on Earth pressed a button, sending a message to *Viking 1,* 212 million miles away. Three thousand miles above Mars, the lander separated from the rest of the spacecraft (the orbiter) and plunged down toward its target. Four miles above Mars, a parachute opened, slowing the craft's descent from approximately 600 to about 100 miles per hour. Just a mile above Mars, three rocket engines fired to ease the three-legged lander down gently. At 4:53 A.M. Pacific time—an hour before sunrise on the U.S. West Coast—the 1,300-pound lander touched down safely on the surface of Mars.

Inside the auditorium of NASA's Jet Propulsion Laboratory in Pasadena, California, the hundreds of waiting scientists and reporters did not know whether the lander had crashed or arrived in one piece. Radio and TV messages travel through space at 186,282 miles per second (the speed of light). Since Mars was 212 million miles from Earth, the huge crowd at the laboratory had to wait 19 minutes to learn the fate of the lander.

At 5:12 A.M. a signal from the lander was received on Earth: The lander had become the first spacecraft from our planet to make a successful descent onto Mars. [Figure 4]

Within a minute of the lander's arrival, one of its television cameras began scanning the Martian scenery. The world watched in awe as the first pictures from the surface of Mars were beamed to their home television screens. Viewers saw a rock-and-pebble-strewn surface, with sand dunes and ridges in the distance. A few weeks later, on September 3, 1976, the *Viking 2* lander arrived and beamed similar pictures Earthward. While the landers photographed Mars from its surface, the orbiters took pictures from high overhead. One revelation of the *Viking* pictures was that pink and red soil particles blown about in the air make Mars's daytime sky pink and its sunset blue—the opposite of Earth with its blue sky and pink sunsets. The *Viking* mission also gathered evidence that Mars looks red because a process called *oxidation* has rusted and reddened the iron-rich rocks on its surface, much as certain metals rust on Earth.

The general feeling among scientists was that if Mars had any life at all, it was probably limited to microbes. By definition, microbes (from Greek words meaning "small life") cannot be seen without a microscope, so the lander cameras could not have revealed them. The cameras could have revealed animals, though—if any existed. Carl Sagan was said to be the only *Viking* scientist who believed in this possibility. He coined a name for them—*macrobes* (from Greek words meaning "large life")—and pointed out that in Earth's cold, dry areas, animals tend to be large in order to retain warmth and moisture. For example, seals, reindeer, and polar bears are found around Earth's polar regions. Despite their size, Martian animals could be difficult to recognize, Sagan argued, for they might be red to blend in with the landscape, or even resemble rocks. Unless someone carefully examined the pictures, Martian animals could be overlooked.

Sagan was on the *Viking* lander "imaging team," which examined the 5,000 pictures transmitted from the surface of Mars. While other team members analyzed photographs to learn more about Mars's rocks and soil, Sagan studied them for signs of animal life. Adding that it would be a shame if remnants of an ancient Martian civilization escaped our notice because nobody bothered to look, he convinced NASA to assign him to hunt for such evidence on the 51,000 orbiter pictures. "*Someone* should look for these things," he told scientists who thought he was wasting his time.

Sagan found no evidence of animals or ancient Martian monuments. Still, this did not mean that they didn't exist, for the lander cameras took pictures of only one twenty-millionth of Mars's surface, and perhaps the orbiters were too high to discern artificial structures. Sagan insisted that more detailed explorations were needed to prove or disprove the existence of higher life-forms on Mars.

For a short time, many people thought that the mission actually *had* found evidence of a Martian civilization. On July 24, a *Viking* scientist studying pictures of Mars's surface noted a B-shaped formation on a rock. He didn't say that a *B* was etched onto the rock—just that a shape in the rock resembled the letter. Before you could say "Percival Lowell," reporters studying TV monitors at the Jet Propulsion Laboratory thought they saw the *B* as well as a *G* along with the numbers *2, 3,* and *4* carved onto the rock. The TV networks ran news bulletins about the "discovery," momentarily convincing millions of viewers that the Martians had written us messages.

The scientist who had spotted the B-shaped formation explained that there were no letters and numbers, only indistinct shadows. However, there was widespread distrust

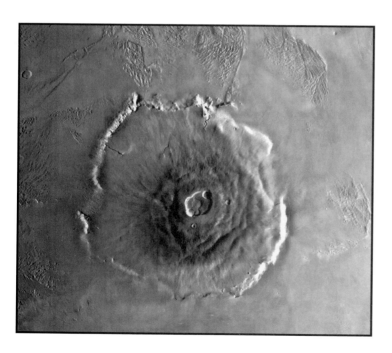

Viking **image of Olympus Mons, the highest known mountain in the Solar System**

of the government at this time. Two years earlier, in 1974, President Richard Nixon had resigned because of a scandal; and in 1973, the United States had pulled out of the Vietnam War, which many Americans felt the government had mismanaged. So, when the scientist offered his explanation, a rumor spread that the *Viking* mission had found Martians but that our government was covering it up to prevent a massive panic. Certain formations photographed by the orbiters sparked even stranger reports that will be mentioned later. Although this was 1976, Lowell's views were still so entrenched in the public mind that, with one B-shaped shadow, the Martians lived again!

While Sagan's projects and the so-called Martian rock inscriptions were more exciting to the public, at the heart of the *Viking* mission were three experiments that attempted a less spectacular search for life. Called the *pyrolytic release experiment,* the *labeled release experiment,* and the *gas exchange experiment,* they involved testing the Martian soil with miniature laboratories for signs of microbial activity.

Pyrolytic refers to chemical changes caused by heat. On Earth, exposure to sunlight causes chemical changes in living things. In the pyrolytic release experiment, a sample of Martian soil was placed inside a chamber and exposed to a sunlamp that simulated sunlight on Mars. If chemical changes characteristic of living things were detected, it could be evidence of life.

But life can exist in the dark, too. The labeled release experiment was designed to search for signs of microbes in a dark environment. A Martian soil sample was placed in an unlit container and given nutrients, or foods, containing a radioactive substance called *carbon 14*. The experiment was equipped with a *Geiger counter*—an instrument that detects radioactive substances. If microbes in the soil consumed the nutrients, carbon-14 gas could be released that might be traced by the Geiger counter.

On Earth, living things exchange gases with the atmosphere. Plants take in carbon dioxide and give off oxygen. People breathe in

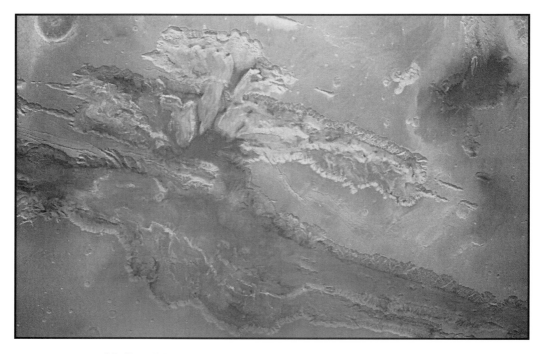

**Valles Marineris, the three-thousand-mile-long
"Grand Canyon of Mars"**

oxygen and release carbon dioxide. The gas exchange experiment was nicknamed the "chicken soup experiment" because it treated the soil sample to a broth composed of water and rich nutrients. If living things in the soil consumed the broth, they might give off gases that could be analyzed by an instrument called a *gas chromatograph mass spectrometer.*

And the outcome? The scientists became excited about their results, which at times seemed to indicate that the Martian soil might contain live organisms. At a press conference, it was announced that it looked "very much like a biological signal," meaning primitive life, had been discovered on Mars.

Doubt soon cast its shadow over these conclusions, though, as it began to appear that chemicals in the Martian soil were mimicking life and that no microbes were present. Today, nearly all scientists feel that the *Viking* mission's experiments show a "chemical reaction" rather than biological activity, explained Dr. Gerald Soffen, the *Viking* project director. Despite the passage of nearly twenty-five years, Dr. Soffen still expresses disappointment over "our inability to find any organics. Personally I don't believe there is any life on the surface of Mars because I think our experiments would have detected evidence of it," he says. However, a few scientists haven't dismissed the possibility that the experiments did in fact show a "biological signal."

While the landers studied the planet's surface, the *Viking* orbiter photographs provided some surprises. One involved the polar caps. Although composed largely of frozen carbon dioxide, the caps also seem to contain frozen water. This raised the hopes of people like Carl Sagan who thought that Mars might have a few warm spots with liquid water.

The *Viking* mission ended operations in the early 1980s. Thousands of *Viking* pictures became available to the public. Some people who looked at them thought certain images showed artificial structures built by ancient Martians. The best known of these, called the "Mars Face," is thought by some people to be a monument in the form of a huge head.

It has also been claimed that an ancient city and pyramids appear in *Viking* images of Mars. However, virtually all scientists agree that the pictures show nothing unnatural and point out that if you look at enough rock formations, you are bound to find a few that resemble familiar objects.

Still, Mars has surprised us so often that perhaps we should file the supposed ancient Martian monuments with the many other questions that the *Viking* mission left unanswered. Could the few scientists who think there are microbes in the Martian soil be right? If not on the

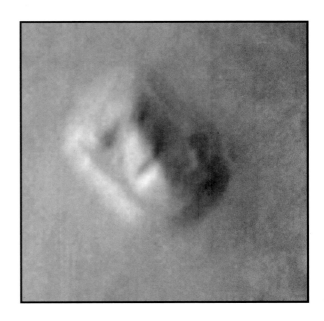

The "Mars Face"

planet's surface, do microbes live deep underground? Does Mars have a few warm spots with liquid water and some form of life? Are fossils of plants and animals buried beneath Mars's surface?

Common sense tells us that to answer any of these questions, we must either bring pieces of Mars back to Earth or send astronauts to the planet. But then, in 1996, scientists announced that they had found a new and unexpected way to search for life on Mars.

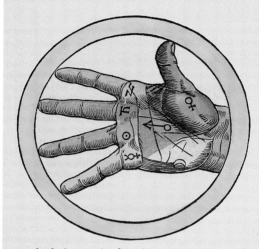

Top left: Figure 1. Picture from a 1534 book illustrating palmistry. The triangular area in the center of the palm is known as the Plain of Mars.

Top right: Figure 2. An illustration from 1660 depicting Earth and the other planets orbiting the Sun

Bottom: Figure 3. Telescopic view of the center of the Milky Way Galaxy

Top: Figure 4. *Viking* orbiter view of Mars

Left: Figure 5. Artist's idea of an asteroid slamming into Mars

Opposite top: Figure 6. If Mars has fossils, dry lake beds (such as the formation at center) should be likely places to find them.

Opposite bottom: Figure 7. *Sojourner,* the "two-foot geologist"

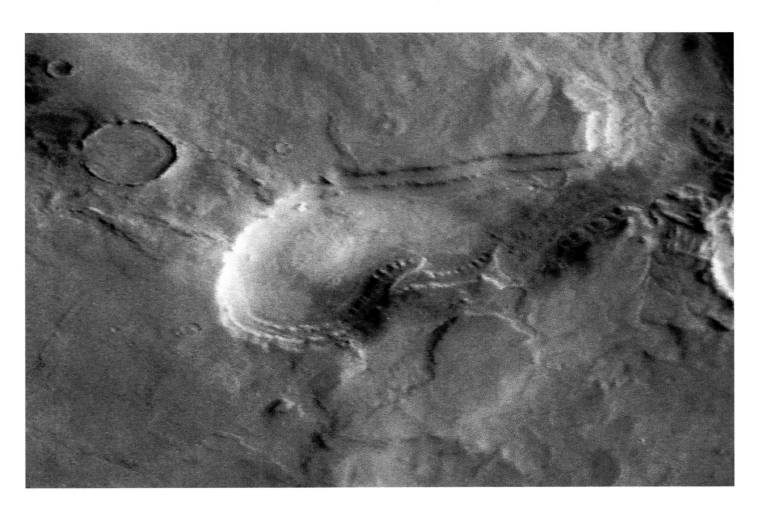

Figure 8. Artist's picture of a rover picking up a piece of Mars as part of the Mars Sample Return Mission that may be launched in 2005.

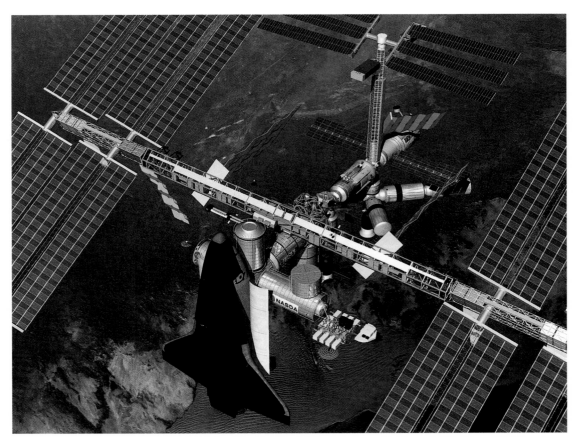

Figure 9. Artist's view of an international space station. A Mars mission involving humans could be assembled and launched from a space station.

Top: **Figure 10.** Artist's portrayal of explorers on Mars

Bottom: **Figure 11.** This artistic rendition shows future Mars settlers setting up an apparatus that will use the Sun's energy to create electricity.

Top: Figure 12. Artist's idea of astronauts working on Phobos. According to one futuristic plan, dark materials from Phobos could be spread over Mars's South Pole, helping to warm the planet.

Left: Figure 13. In this artist's view of a terraformed Mars of the future, the planet resembles Earth.

Opposite top left: Figure 14. More than 1,500 galaxies, as far away as 19 billion light-years, are shown in this 1995 Hubble Space Telescope photograph.

Opposite top right: Figure 15. This amazing photo, taken by a hundred-inch reflector in Chile, shows material around a star called Beta Pictoris. The material could be leftover debris from the formation of planets too small and dim for us to see.

Opposite right: Figure 16. Artist's rendition of a space colony

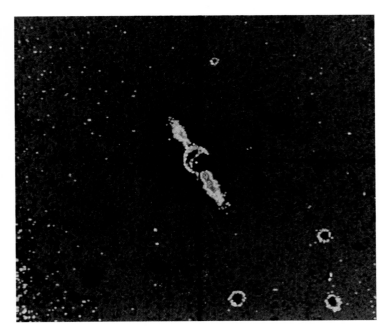

Top: **Figure 17.** Artist's vision of a soccer game in a future Mars colony

Left: **Figure 18.** In this artist's futuristic view, astronauts are preparing to protect themselves from a dust storm on the Red Planet.

eight

Are We Martians?

♂ **Largely because of** disappointment in the *Viking* results, interest in Mars dwindled in the 1980s and early 1990s. The United States, Russia, Japan, and the European Space Agency (a group of European nations involved in space exploration) sent spacecraft to study such objects as Halley's Comet, Venus, Jupiter, and the Sun, yet twenty years passed and not a single probe was landed on Mars following the arrival of the *Vikings* in 1976.

Dr. Gerald Soffen, who had directed the *Viking* project, admits that even he lost interest in Mars. "After *Viking,* most of the scientists who had been involved in the mission including myself gave up on the idea of discovering life on Mars in our own time, and so we became interested in other things. For a number of years few scientists did anything involving life on Mars. All that changed in 1996."

That year, there was a tremendous burst of interest in the Red Planet. Headlines announced that Mars was the subject of the DISCOVERY OF THE CENTURY, astronomers spun new theories about the planet, and

Martian mania awoke from a long slumber. Remarkably, the revived interest in Mars was due mainly to a potato-sized, green rock found near the Earth's South Pole.

Countless pieces of rock and metal called *meteoroids* float through the Solar System. Each day, millions of meteoroids cross the Earth's path and burn up high in our atmosphere, creating streaks across the sky known as *meteors,* or *shooting stars.* Most meteors are the result of meteoroids roughly the size of a grain of sand burning up high above our planet. Some brighter meteors are about the size of a pea. Now and then, a meteoroid the size of a softball or even a truck crosses Earth's path. When that occurs, pieces of the meteoroid may hit our planet. Called *meteorites,* these visitors from space have been found around the world and are exhibited in many museums.

At least thirteen meteorites found on Earth are pieces of Mars.

How can we tell that a meteorite came from the Red Planet? Among other things, the *Viking* landers revealed the makeup of Mars's atmosphere, which includes large amounts of carbon dioxide and small amounts of such gases as nitrogen, argon, and oxygen. Mars's atmosphere is distinct from that of other bodies in the Solar System and is a kind of signature of the planet. Rocks on a planet can contain bubbles that trap some of the surrounding gases. The Martian meteorites reveal their place of origin because they contain trapped gases that closely match the composition of Mars's atmosphere.

How can pieces of Mars wind up on Earth? Each planet has an *escape velocity*—the speed at which a moving object will break free of the planet's gravitational field and head out into space. The more massive a planet is, the stronger is its gravitational field and the faster an object must travel to escape. A rocket traveling at Earth's escape velocity—7 miles per second, or 25,000 miles per hour—will break free of our planet's gravitation and enter interplanetary space. Less massive than Earth, Mars has an escape velocity of 3 miles per second, or 11,000 miles per hour.

Antarctic field camp of U.S. meteorite hunters

We know that Mars has been repeatedly struck by such objects as asteroids and huge meteorites, because we can see the craters that these impacts have made. Astronomers believe that, long ago, several objects hit Mars with enough force to jar pieces of the planet loose and send them flying at more than 3 miles per second—fast enough to launch them off the Red Planet and into space.

United States Antarctic meteorite team collecting a meteorite

Some of the pieces of Mars headed our way and were eventually pulled down to Earth by our planet's gravitation. These Martian meteorites, or chunks of Mars, are called SNCs, for the first letters of the names of places where three of them were found: *S*hergotty (India), *N*akhla (Egypt), and *C*hassigny (France).

SNC meteorites contain clues about Mars's past. Minerals in some SNCs show that, back when they were part of Mars, the rocks were at times covered by salty water. This indicates that Mars may have had oceans as well as rivers, and it further supports the theory that the planet was formerly a warm, wet world that may have supported life.

Each year, the National Science Foundation, a U.S. government agency, sends meteorite hunters to Antarctica, the ice-covered continent surrounding the South Pole. On December 27, 1984, the six members of an Antarctic meteorite team went snowmobiling through a beautiful area near the South Pole called the Allan Hills. Suddenly geologist Roberta Score spotted a bright green rock in the ice. "This is a really weird rock!" she thought, wrapping the $4\frac{1}{2}$-pound object in a plastic bag. Just how weird it was no one would realize for quite a while.

The rock was taken to NASA's Johnson Space Center in Houston, Texas, where it was cleaned and examined. Scientists decided that it was a common type of meteorite that had originated in the region between Mars and Jupiter. They named it ALH84001 (because it was found in the *Allan Hills* in *1984* and was meteorite number *1* found there that year). The meteorite was placed in a vault and ignored for nearly ten years.

Then, in 1993, NASA scientist David Mittlefehldt did tests on ALH84001. From the minerals he found in the meteorite, Mittlefehldt suspected that it was from Mars. Further tests revealed that the gases trapped within the rock bore the signature of the Martian atmosphere. A team of scientists from NASA and several universities began scrutinizing the meteorite. Through their painstaking detective work, the history of the "Mars rock" was deciphered.

All rocks contain traces of radioactive elements that over time, and at a certain rate, break down into other elements. By measuring the amounts of these elements, the ages of most rocks can be determined. ALH84001 was found to be 4.5 billion years old—far older than all other known SNCs. The Solar System was formed about 4.6 billion years ago, so this means that the meteorite dates back to when Mars was newly formed.

When an object is in space, particles called *cosmic rays* strike it and create certain changes within it. By analyzing these changes, scientists can tell how long an object has been in space. The cosmic ray record helped scientists determine that the Mars rock spent about 16 million years in space. In addition, chemical analysis of its outer layers showed that the rock landed in Antarctica about 13,000 years ago.

Piecing together the

The "Mars rock," ALH84001

clues, scientists determined what had occurred. Apparently the rock sat on Mars for more than 4.4 billion years. About 16 million years ago—a recent era in the history of our Solar System—an asteroid or giant meteorite struck Mars, hurling the rock into space. The piece of Mars wandered through the Solar System for most of those 16 million years. Then about 13,000 years ago—when human beings still lived in caves—the rock came within reach of Earth's gravitation. It plunged through our atmosphere, creating a brilliant flash. A large chunk of the meteorite that did not burn up landed on the Antarctic ice sheet. Ice and snow covered the object, but the glaciers' movements eventually brought it to the surface, where Roberta Score noticed it in 1984.

Scanning the rock with a powerful instrument called an *electron microscope,* scientists made a startling discovery. The rock contains many tube-shaped formations, so small that 250,000 of them strung end to end would cover only an inch. Yet these tiny formations may have once been alive. They resemble microfossils (microscopic remains) of early bacteria found on Earth, except that they are about one hundred times smaller.

Besides the bacteria-like shapes, the rock contains three other clues indicating that microbes may have once lived inside it.

First, scientists bombarded pieces of ALH84001 with lasers to identify the chemicals in the meteorite and found that they contain PAHs—*polycyclic aromatic hydrocarbons.* Black tarry substances will form on the outside of food such as chicken that is placed too near the charcoal on a barbecue grill. Those substances are PAHs. One way they are created is by the decay of microbes, which may have been how the Mars rock's PAHs originated.

Second, cracks in the meteorite were found to contain *carbonates.* Composed of carbon and oxygen, these substances are often associated with life-forms. Bones and teeth, for example, contain carbonates. The Mars rock's carbonates are similar in texture and size to carbonates formed on Earth with the help of bacteria. Using three dif-

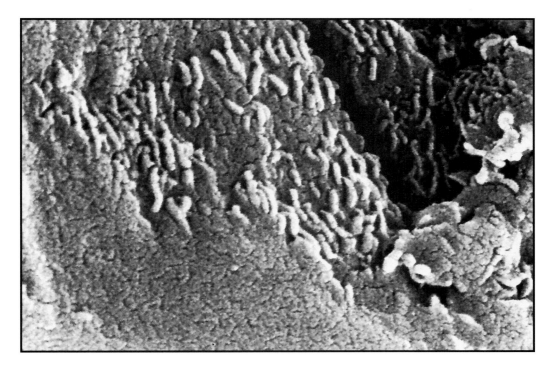

Tube-shaped formations in ALH84001. Some people think they are microfossils of bacteria-like organisms from Mars.

ferent methods, scientists determined that the Mars rock's carbonates date back 3.6 billion years. This suggests that the biological activity in the rock occurred long ago when it was on Mars, rather than after it arrived on Earth.

Finally, minerals associated with life on Earth were detected in the Mars rock. These include the magnetic substances pyrrhotite and magnetite—iron minerals that form within many organisms on Earth. In fact, the combination of minerals found in the Mars rock is rarely seen on Earth *unless* living organisms have been present.

On August 7, 1996, the nine-member scientific team that had analyzed the rock announced its findings at a press conference in Washington, D.C. The scientists admitted that each of the four clues—the bacteria-like shapes, the PAHs, the carbonates, and the minerals associated with life—could have nonbiological explanations. Yet they felt that, taken together, the four clues offered "circumstantial [likely but not definite] evidence" that Mars once had primitive life.

Because this would be the first life ever discovered beyond Earth, the announcement made worldwide headlines. In its front-page story DISCOVERY WOULD EQUAL FINDING THE NEW WORLD, *USA Today* declared: "A finding of life on Mars might end up being the main thing the 20th Century is remembered for." The *Chicago Tribune* predicted: "If it proves true, the discovery would surely rank as one of the scientific achievements of our age." *Newsweek* magazine's story COME IN, MARS, quoted a space scientist as saying: "This is the biggest thing that has ever happened!" The news raised hopes that Mars once had more advanced life and that it may have life today. Stanford University chemist Richard Zare, a member of the ALH84001 scientific team, told *Astronomy* magazine: "It's really quite conceivable that one could go to Mars and find some life-forms that are still alive, because I imagine there are some places with water and hot spots underground."

The Mars rock has rekindled interest in the subject of life on Mars among scientists who had, as Dr. Gerald Soffen said, "given up" the quest, and it has inspired many younger astronomers to think about the Red Planet for the first time. Moreover, explains Dr. Soffen, "The Mars rock has helped open a new field—astrobiology." Also called *exobiology*, this science involves the search for life beyond Earth and the study of the conditions necessary for the development of life.

There was more exciting news in November of 1996, when three British scientists announced that they had found evidence of microbial remains in another Martian meteorite recovered from Antarctica. "This is a smoking gun for life on Mars"—meaning more circumstantial evidence—said Ian Wright, one of the scientists. The British and American meteorites greatly differ in age. The life in ALH84001 is believed to date back 3.6 billion years—the early days of our Solar System. The British meteorite is thought to be only 180 million years old. If Mars had life during this relatively recent period, the odds increase that it has live organisms today.

But by early 1997, a number of scientists had begun to doubt that the two Mars rocks contain evidence of life. The doubters claim that the tube-shaped formations are only mineral crystals and have nothing to do with bacteria. The other so-called clues also have strictly mineral explanations, they add. University of Tennessee geologist Dr. Harry McSween felt so badly about ruining the fun that he said: "It makes me feel like the Grinch, stealing everybody's Martians!"

As in the days of "canalists" and "anti-canalists," there are now what we might call "microfossilists" and "anti-microfossilists." Which side is right about the Mars rocks? NASA is making fragments of meteorite ALH84001 available to scientists around the world, so that they can be further studied for signs of past life.

To learn more about what it would mean if we proved that Mars once had microorganisms, I spent two days at Lowell Observatory in October 1997 with Dr. John Stansberry and Dr. John Spencer, astronomers who study the Solar System. Stansberry took me to Percival Lowell's tomb, a small round building with a blue glass dome that resembles a miniature observatory. "Percival Lowell took the idea of ETs [extraterrestrials] and showed us a place—Mars—where we can embody the idea," says Stansberry, a thirty-five-year-old Colorado native. "Although scientists look back at him as a bit of a crackpot, he advanced the concept of life beyond Earth in the popular mind."

Sitting before a globe of Mars in a research building, Stansberry then provided a brief tour of the planet. "The two most important aspects of Mars are that it is a desert and it is extremely cold. If you condensed all the water from Mars's atmosphere, you'd have only a few millimeters of liquid water covering the planet's surface. Typical temperatures on Mars are about minus one hundred degrees Fahrenheit. Walking around in your space suit you would see rust-colored ground. The sky would look orangish-brown-pink, with lots of windblown reddish dust in it. The landscape has great variety—dry riverbeds, boulders scattered about long ago by water, craters, mountains larger than the state of Hawaii, and canyons deeper than any on Earth."

Dr. John Spencer, a forty-year-old English-born astronomer, continued the minitour of Mars. "The areas in the United States Mars looks most like are Death Valley or the Mojave Desert [both in California]. There is even a place in Death Valley called Mars Hill because it looks so much like Mars. In places you would see vast sand dunes on Mars. The dust on the ground might be hundreds of feet thick in places, but I'd imagine it is compact enough to walk on without sinking in."

Is there life on Mars? Stansberry and Spencer agree that, while the meteorites show signs of having contained primitive organisms, the case isn't yet proven. "The evidence is intriguing, but not compelling," says Dr. Spencer. Both astronomers also think that, regardless of the outcome with the meteorites, Mars may have once had life and could still have it today.

"Recently we have found living microorganisms in places on Earth that we once thought were too harsh to support life, so we now think it more likely that microorganisms live on Mars," Stansberry explains. "As we go deeper into the ground on Mars, the temperature rises. It is reasonable to think that at a certain depth the temperature rises above thirty-two degrees Fahrenheit—where you can have liquid water. There could be aquifers [underground pools of water] down there with live bacteria in them."

The two astronomers think that there may be fossils of more advanced life-forms on Mars. "Conceivably Mars had more advanced life than bacteria when it had lots of water and was warmer than it is today," says Stansberry. "That would be about three and a half billion years ago when Mars was about a billion years old."

Discovering any organisms on Mars—fossilized or alive—would do far more than show us that life has existed on our neighbor planet, Stansberry and Spencer explain. It could help us determine whether life in the Universe is plentiful or rare. Currently Earth is the only planet that we know has life. "With just one sample," explains Dr. Spencer, "we can't tell whether life is incredibly difficult to create and we happen to live on the only planet with perfect conditions. But if life began on two planets that happen to be next to each other and aren't very similar, then it would appear that the Universe is teeming with life."

"Mars could be the key to the entire SETI question," adds Dr. Stansberry, referring to the *Search* for *Extra*terrestrial *Intelligence.* "Of the Sun's nine planets, we know that Mercury and Venus are too hot to support life. Those beyond Mars—Jupiter, Saturn, Uranus, Neptune, and Pluto—are too cold. If life actually evolved on the only two of the Sun's planets that seem capable of supporting life [Earth and Mars], then we can apply these results to planets around other stars and conclude that the chances of life everywhere in the Universe are excellent."

The two Lowell Observatory astronomers went on to say that the discovery of even simple organisms on Mars might reveal that Martians exist and that we can see them by looking in the mirror. As John Stansberry phrases it: "*We* could be the little green men—the Martians."

The theory that we might be Martians has been gaining credibility among scientists in the past few years. To understand why, it helps to know about two other theories. The first is the theory of evolution, which most scientists believe explains how various organisms developed on Earth. Originated in the 1800s, this theory starts with the idea that life on Earth began more than three billion years ago with a simple type of organism such as bacteria. Over the ages, these one-celled organisms evolved—or developed—into more complex life-forms. These, in turn, evolved into the living things that inhabit our planet today—roses, giraffes, chimpanzees, human beings, and thousands of other organisms. Any life on other planets might also gradually evolve from simpler to more complex organisms.

But how did these first simple organisms originate on Earth to begin with? Most scientists think it happened through a series of chemical reactions that took place in our oceans and atmosphere. In 1907, Svante August Arrhenius, a Nobel Prize–winning chemist from Sweden, proposed a different idea—the *panspermia* theory—in his book *Worlds in the Making*. Spores float through the Universe from planet to planet, claimed Arrhenius. Produced by bacteria and other simple organisms, spores can withstand harsh conditions for long periods of time and then transform themselves back into the original organisms once conditions improve. Arrhenius believed that the spores land on countless planets, starting the evolutionary process that in at least one case resulted in intelligent beings (ourselves). Arrhenius concluded his book by asserting that, if his theory was correct: "All organic beings in the whole Universe are related to one another."

The theory that we may be Martians involves aspects of the evolution and panspermia ideas. The theory proposes that, several billion years ago, before Earth had any life, spores landed on Mars, changed back into microbes, and began evolving into higher life-forms. At a time when life flourished on Mars, an asteroid or other large object slammed into the Red Planet, dislodging rocks and sending them toward Earth. Burrowed deep inside cracks in these ejected Martian rocks were tiny hitchhikers: microbes. Perhaps by forming spores, the microbes survived the incredibly harsh conditions of space. After landing on Earth, the spores changed back into active microbes. If this actually happened, the Martian microbes may have been the original organisms from which all life on Earth—including ourselves—evolved. [Figure 5]

A questionable part of the theory is whether organisms hitchhiking in rocks could endure the interplanetary journey. "We don't know if they could survive the trip through space or the impact of landing on another planet," Dr. Spencer explains. Assuming they could, the sequence of events could be reversed. Life could have started on Earth and been carried to Mars in rocks knocked off of our planet. The Mars-to-Earth scenario seems more likely, however, because, as Stansberry points out, "It is easier for things to be knocked off Mars than off Earth" due to the Red Planet's weaker gravitation.

If we found life on Mars, we would have at least three possibilities to consider, Dr. Spencer continues. "Life jumped from Mars to Earth. It jumped from Earth to Mars. Or it began independently on both planets." The first possibility is intriguing because it would be so strange to trace our evolutionary family tree to Mars, but scientists would be most excited if life began independently on the two planets. The reason relates to the question of whether life in the Universe is plentiful or rare. If life jumped from Mars to Earth, it would only show that, once begun, life is contagious. But if life started independently on both planets, it would show that life tends to occur naturally when given a chance.

Should we ever find Martian organisms, we may be able to determine whether life on Mars began independently of life on Earth.

All living things are made of units called *cells*. Bacteria have one cell, while human beings are composed of trillions of cells. Cells contain *deoxyribonucleic acid,* a genetic material called DNA for short. So minuscule that 10 million threads of it measure only an inch, DNA is so important that it is nicknamed "the code of life." An organism's DNA determines its identity. A bee's DNA differs from a chimpanzee's, and human DNA differs from that of an ant, an oak tree, or a bacterium.

Despite variations from organism to organism, the threads of DNA of all Earth's living things share certain chemical patterns. This is probably because all living things on our planet are related in basic ways, having evolved from a simple organism that branched out into more complex forms. Life on another planet would take its own evolutionary route and should have DNA distinguishable from that of all Earth life. If organisms on Earth and Mars had dissimilar DNA, we could conclude that life probably developed independently on the two worlds. On the other hand, if organisms on Mars and Earth had similar DNA, life may have begun first on one planet and later been transplanted to the other.

Imagine that we eventually discover live organisms, or well-preserved dead organisms, on Mars. "We could extract the DNA from the Martian organisms, study it, and determine whether the organisms developed independently of life on Earth," explains Dr. Spencer.

What if the DNA was a close match? How would we know whether Martian life jumped to Earth, or vice versa? We might be able to tell by calculating the age of the oldest microfossils we find on Mars. "Earth's oldest life began when our planet was about a billion and a half years old"—about three billion years ago, Dr. Stansberry says. If the DNA of organisms on the two planets was similar—and if we found evidence of Martian life dating back *four* billion years—it could mean that we evolved from organisms from Mars.

Of course, all this is just speculation. As of 1999, we have nothing that could definitely be said to have lived on Mars. To find well-preserved, or living, Martian organisms whose DNA we can study, we will probably have to send explorers to the Red Planet.

Plans are now being made to do just that.

nine

People Land on Mars

♂ **Around the year** 2020, aliens will land on Mars. They will wear multilayered, tightly bound suits. Large bubbles will cover their heads. On their backs will be the gas supplies they need to breathe. Only the fact that they have two legs and two arms will reveal that these creatures are Earthlings.

Most people are surprised to learn that we already have the technology to land astronauts on the Red Planet.

While in Flagstaff, I visited the United States Geological Survey (USGS) office. Traditionally the USGS has studied Earth's geology—its rocks, mountains, and other features. Since 1963, it has expanded to aid NASA in investigating other worlds, including Mars. In the process, the USGS has helped create a new science called *astrogeology,* which is the study of the geology of heavenly bodies.

"Yes, we are capable of landing people on Mars," explains Dr. Lisa R. Gaddis, a USGS astrogeologist involved in the long-term program to send astronauts to the Red Planet. We have the designs for the rockets, space suits, fuel, and other necessities. "We're just being careful because the mission involves people," she says. To make the expedition as safe and efficient as possible, scientists like Dr. Gaddis are trying to determine the best places to land and search for life. Not only must we be certain that we can launch astronauts to Mars, but we must also be able to bring them home safely. All of this takes years of preparation.

Although no date has been set, the talk around NASA is that the first human expedition to Mars may occur in 2011 or 2018. To pave the way, NASA is sending a series of probes to Mars. The plan calls for launches of robotic craft in 1996, 1998, 2001, 2003, and 2005, with subsequent missions approximately every two years when Earth and Mars are close together.

The 1996 "Window of Opportunity"

Mars Global Surveyor (MGS) was launched in late 1996 and reached Mars in September of 1997. In April 1999, after spending a year and a half achieving the proper orbit, it began to map the Red Planet from a height of about 250 miles. Capable of imaging features less than 10 feet across, *MGS* is scheduled to map Mars until early in the year 2001. *MGS* may locate promising sites for astronauts to search for signs of life in years to come. These include ancient dry lake beds, which are good spots for fossil hunting, and hot springs of water, where live microbes might conceivably be found. [Figure 6]

Mars Pathfinder, the other U.S. spacecraft launched to Mars in 1996, landed in a rock-strewn plain called Ares Vallis on July 4, 1997. *Pathfinder* carried a 22-pound vehicle named *Sojourner* that resembled a toy truck. When this six-wheeled vehicle rolled down a ramp, it became the first rover to explore another planet. Moving at a top speed of one-fortieth of a mile per hour (the pace of a snail), *Sojourner* had the task of analyzing the composition of Martian rocks. [Figure 7]

The *Pathfinder-Sojourner* mission lasted three months and was a tremendous success. *Sojourner* traveled 330 feet—roughly the length of a football field—without any disastrous crashes. The mission gathered evidence that, like our planet, Mars seems to be composed of an outer rocky *crust* with a hot layer below it called the *mantle* and a central *core* of extremely hot iron. The hot rock inside Mars may warm underground water, which could provide a comfortable home for live organisms.

Russia also launched a Mars mission in 1996. Russia's *Mars '96* carried two *penetrators*—devices designed to drill as deep as 20 feet beneath the Martian surface and research conditions inside the planet. Shortly after blastoff, however, the probe crashed to Earth, illustrating the importance of solving problems with robotic craft before we send people to Mars.

The 1998 "Window"

"Water is gold on Mars," says Dr. Gerald Soffen. Not only are wet areas the likeliest places to find life, but one day people may use Mars's water to drink, grow crops, and even produce fuel.

Missions that will search for water and examine the planet's atmosphere were launched during the 1998 window of opportunity. Japan launched *Nozomi* (meaning "hope") in 1998. Japan's first probe to Mars, *Nozomi* was scheduled to reach orbit around the red planet in late 1999, but fuel problems will delay arrival until about 2003. *Nozomi* is expected to make detailed studies of Mars's upper atmosphere, and it may also identify water sources on the planet.

The U.S. *Mars Surveyor '98* mission involves two craft, both scheduled to arrive in 1999. The *'98 Orbiter* will study Mars's atmosphere and create global weather maps of the planet. The *'98 Lander* will descend on Mars's South Pole and extend a robotic arm that will scoop up snow and soil for analysis. Together, the *'98 Orbiter* and *Lander* may reveal how much water Mars has in its atmosphere and at its poles.

The "Martian Century" Begins

Some scientists predict that the twenty-first century will become known as "the Martian century" because human beings will explore and colonize the Red Planet. Missions early in the century will move us closer to these goals.

The United States expects to launch its *Mars Surveyor 2001* mission in the spring of 2001. The *2001 Lander* will release a rover that may travel several miles collecting soil and rock samples. The *2001 Lander* will also include a miniature chemical plant that will test techniques for making rocket fuel and oxygen by processing Martian atmospheric gases. If this can be done, as engineers expect, human visitors to Mars won't have to bring along as much oxygen to breathe or as much rocket fuel for the return trip to Earth. They will make these substances on Mars.

The farther we gaze into the future, the more uncertain it becomes that a mission will be carried out as planned. Information gathered by a previous mission could change our plans, or delays might occur. But currently NASA expects that its 2003 mission to Mars will be similar to that of 2001. More rock and soil samples will be collected, perhaps with the help of the European Space Agency.

The soil and rocks collected in 2001 and 2003 will remain on Mars, awaiting one of the most exciting events in the history of space travel: the *Mars Sample Return Mission,* scheduled for launch in 2005. A rover released by the 2005 landing craft will travel to either the 2001 or 2003 site and pick up the soil and rock samples. The samples will be rocketed up to the orbiter and transferred to a spacecraft that will return them to Earth in 2008. [Figure 8]

Scientists on Earth will be eager to examine the pieces of Mars, but they will have to be patient. Although we were nearly certain that the Moon was lifeless, the *Apollo 11* astronauts who made the first human Moon landing in 1969 were isolated for eighteen days after returning to Earth. The quarantine wasn't lifted until scientists were satisfied that the astronauts and their samples contained no harmful Moon organisms. Similarly, the Mars samples will be examined to make sure they contain no dangerous microbes before being released for study.

First People on Mars!

While scientists generally agree that bacteria may have lived on Mars, they disagree about the possibility of plants and animals. Some say that Mars never had the proper conditions to support higher life-forms. Others side with planetary scientist Dr. Susan Sakimoto of NASA's Goddard Space Flight Center in Greenbelt, Maryland, who says: "I think there is a good chance Mars could have supported plant or simple animal life in the past—perhaps when liquid water was present on or close to the surface, and the atmosphere was thicker."

No matter what their opinion about life on Mars, scientists agree on two points. We won't find fossils on Mars if we don't look, and human beings will be more effective than probes at searching for them.

Even on Earth, where dinosaurs, saber-toothed tigers, giant ferns, and millions of other kinds of organisms have lived and died, finding a fossil is rare. To begin with, fossils, which are the preserved remains of living things, are not easily formed. An organism must be covered by such substances as mud and sand at just the right time. It must lie buried over a long period and eventually be uncovered or brought near the surface by such forces as wind, water, and the wearing away of rock. Finally, someone or something must go to just the right place to dig out or pick up the fossil.

People on Mars could drill deeper and recognize signs of past life more effectively than could robots. Furthermore, no machine can match our nimble fingers at searching for delicate fossils, or equal our brains for piecing together clues that can lead to a discovery. Experts calculate that, in a search for Martian life, a human crew would accomplish in one year what would take robot devices 100 years to achieve.

Fossil hunting isn't the only reason people will go to Mars. Just as looking at someone's vacation photos isn't as exciting as visiting a place oneself, we want to see Mars through human eyes and not just through the eyes of cameras. "If humans are anything, we are explorers, and we are curious," says Dr. Gerald Soffen. "Our curiosity will drive us to send people to Mars."

A young reader of this book may be among the first Mars explorers. If the first crew departs for Mars in 2018 and its members are thirty to thirty-four years old, those future astronauts would be twelve to sixteen years old as of the year 2000.

It happens that my twelve-year-old pen pal, Stephanie Meyer of White Bear Lake, Minnesota, hopes to become an astronaut. I asked Stephanie if she would like to visit Mars one day, and she wrote back: "I would love to go to Mars! Scientists are already trying to find a way to send people there. It is cold, but a space suit would keep me warm. I know it would be risky to go, but space is awe-inspiring and thrilling, and there isn't a better way to learn about Mars than to go there. I think that maybe there was life on Mars a long time ago, but not anymore." Still, she adds, "I think it would be really cool to meet a Martian, if they were peaceful."

What qualities will Stephanie or another young person need in order to be chosen for the first Mars expedition? To start with, the "Marsonauts" (as I call them) will have to be physically and mentally strong to endure the two- or three-year mission. They will have to be able to withstand months of traveling through space, weeks on a cold, practically airless planet, and more months returning to Earth. They will need to think quickly and calmly in emergencies and work harmoniously with a small group of people who will be their only companions for several years. Each crew member will also have to be an expert in at least one field. For example, a doctor will be needed—actually two doctors, in case one of them becomes ill or injured. Likewise, there should be two pilots who can fly the spacecraft, two scientists to conduct a search for life on Mars, two engineers to maintain the craft and equipment, at least two drivers for the Mars rover, a mission commander, and several people who can do such things as prepare food in space. The crew is likely to have about eight people. Because more than eight jobs must be filled, most crew members will perform more than one job.

According to a United Nations space treaty, no nation may claim ownership of a heavenly body, which means that a country can't claim Mars just by going there first. Many people feel that Mars expeditions should and will be international. Although the United States may direct the mission, other nations will probably help build various components, which will include launch rockets, round-trip modules to take the crew to and from Mars orbit, unmanned landers to carry supplies and equipment, descent modules to land the crew on Mars, surface habitats where people can live on the Red Planet, rovers the crew can drive, and ascent modules to lift the crew to the round-trip module that will carry them home. Nations that provide equipment will want to be represented among the crew, so the Marsonauts may come from all over the world.

The committee that chooses the Marsonauts will consider all aspects of the candidates' lives. Alcoholics and drug abusers will be weeded out, and don't expect to become a rover driver if you have lots of speeding tickets. Mars won't have much traffic at first, but a reckless driver could destroy the expedition by driving over a cliff into the Valles Marineris.

Once chosen, the crew will train for several years. They will practice in *simulators*—devices that duplicate the conditions in space vehicles and on Mars. They may also spend several weeks in a space station to become accustomed to living in space.

The spacecraft, supplies, and equipment for the mission may be too heavy to launch from Earth all at once. They may be launched in pieces up to a space station high above our planet—perhaps the *International Space Station,* which the United States and a number of other space-faring nations are building between 1998 and about 2004. This million-pound space station will be about 350 feet across and 300 feet long and will orbit Earth at a height of 220 miles. [Figure 9]

At its closest, Mars is 35 million miles from Earth. Due to fuel considerations, however, the spaceship will follow a curving trajectory that will require a far longer journey than 35 million miles. Depending on how much time and fuel we are willing to consume—and how long we want to stay on Mars—there are several possible routes. One involves a 180-day voyage to Mars, 30 days on the Red Planet, and a 430-day return trip to Earth, for a total mission length of 640 days, or nearly two years. Another route involves a 180-day trip to Mars, 550 days on the planet, and a 180-day return voyage, for a total mission time of 910 days, or two and a half years. Scientists are even considering flying the spaceship past Venus to use that planet's gravitation to "slingshot" the craft to Mars.

Workers at the launch site—whether a space station or another locale—will test the craft thoroughly to make certain it is space-worthy. A few weeks before departure, the crew will be transported to the launch site for final training aboard the craft. Space mechanics will fuel up the craft, and it will be ready for its journey into interplanetary space.

TV cameras will provide Earthlings with a view of nearly every step of the mission. An exciting moment will occur when the craft carrying the Marsonauts ignites its engines and blasts off. The craft will soon reach a speed of just over 7 miles a second, or approximately 26,000 miles per hour.

Without Earth's gravitation to hold them down, the Marsonauts will be weightless aboard their craft, enabling them to hang upside down on the ceiling like bats and balance on one another's fingertips. Zero gravity poses problems for many activities that are routine on Earth, however. The Marsonauts may move about by holding on to handrails and sleep in special bags hung from the ceiling to avoid "floating in their sleep." Air blowers in the bathroom may aim wastes into receptacles. The Marsonauts may drink from containers that resemble baby bottles and eat from plastic-covered containers. Recycling will reduce the amount of supplies that must be brought along. For example, each Marsonaut will consume about 6 pounds of water per day—amounting to 35,000 pounds of water required for an eight-person crew on a two-year expedition. They won't need to bring that much water, though, for the Marsonauts' bodily fluids will be recycled into drinking water.

A danger of space travel is that the Marsonauts' bodies will weaken in zero gravity. They could lose muscle mass and develop bone and heart problems. To keep fit, they will exercise several hours a day on such devices as a stationary bicycle and a treadmill.

The Marsonauts will be the first people to look *down* on the Red Planet. As Mars's towering mountains, deep canyons, and dry riverbeds loom beneath them, the crew enters the descent module, which breaks free from the rest of the spacecraft several hundred miles above the planet. With the help of computers, the commander directs the module down toward the landing target. Slowed by rockets and parachutes, the module descends to an altitude of 15, 5, then 1 mile, 1,000, 500, then just 50 feet above the ground.

Steering clear of obstacles, the commander sets the first human expedition to another planet down upon the surface of Mars.

As a TV camera takes pictures of them and their craft, the crew radios a message to Earth about their safe arrival, but for about ten minutes, people on the home planet do not know the fate of the Marsonauts. Traveling at the speed of light, all TV and radio transmissions between the two planets require several minutes to reach their destination.

After making certain their spacecraft is undamaged, and becoming accustomed to Mars's gravity (which is only about 40 percent that of Earth's but still much more than the zero gravity of space), the crew

Artist's vision of a geologist searching for fossils on Mars

goes to work. Many millions of miles away, Earthlings watch as several Marsonauts put on their space suits and step onto the red surface: the first human beings to walk on Mars.

For the next few weeks or months, the crew's home will be a portion of the descent module called the *habitat*. An unmanned lander may arrive separately to deliver supplies, including the chemical plant that will produce rocket fuel and oxygen from the Martian atmosphere.

Soon after landing, the Marsonauts take out their rover and begin making exploring trips near their base. Part of their assignment is to study the planet's rocks, climate, and atmosphere, but of course the main question on everyone's mind is: Has Mars ever had life?

A camera mounted on the rover allows people on Earth to view the scenery and observe the Marsonauts as they explore. Like the viewers back home on Earth, the Marsonauts are immensely curious—and somewhat apprehensive. They don't expect to meet the Clay People, and they know that conditions on Mars are hostile to higher forms of life as we know it. Still, they have been exposed to so many Martian stories that they can't help wondering what might be lurking behind the next boulder.

An even greater fear is that the crew *won't* find any signs of life. Mars is the only planet in the Solar System besides Earth that seems to have the potential for life (although several moons are possibilities). If Mars is lifeless, we may be in for a long wait before we discover extraterrestrial life.

The Marsonauts will search for life everywhere they can. They will collect rock and soil samples, split open boulders, investigate dried-up river and lake beds, and dig underground. Attached to their rover will be a powerful drilling rig capable of excavating several hundred feet below the surface. The Marsonauts may lower themselves into chasms to look for fossils poking out of the rock layers and go mountain climbing in search of life. [Figure 18]

The expedition scientists will study their samples with a microscope and other instruments. To avoid direct contact with the samples, they will wear gloves and protective clothing. This will safeguard the crew from potentially dangerous organisms and prevent microbes from the Marsonauts' bodies from contaminating the samples.

Russian cosmonaut Valery Polyakov set the record for the longest time in space—439 days—aboard space station *Mir* in 1994–1995. The Mars expedition will last much longer than that, and the astronauts will be much farther from Earth. As the weeks pass and the novelty of living on Mars wears off, the Marsonauts may suffer from "Earth separation anxiety"—a nervousness and depression that some space travelers have already experienced. Certainly there will come a time when they "can't wait" to see the blue oceans and green continents of home.

Finally, departure day arrives. The Marsonauts pack their samples and gear into the ascent module (perhaps the unmanned lander that delivered their supplies) and blast off. They dock with the round-trip module, enter the craft, and head back to Earth, perhaps breathing oxygen and using rocket fuel made on Mars. After a journey that could last more than a year, they arrive at the space station above Earth. There, they and their Mars samples are placed in quarantine until given the all clear to continue on to Earth.

A space shuttle takes the Marsonauts on the last leg of their journey home. Once on Earth, they may need to be carried on stretchers to mission headquarters, for they have experienced zero or reduced gravity for so long that they feel like Earth's gravitation is sucking them down into the ground.

TV appearances, parades, and speaking tours await the Marsonauts. For years, scientists on Earth will use the most sophisticated instruments in existence to search for life in the hundreds of pounds of samples that the Marsonauts have brought back. Will they find microbes or fossils in the samples? Could the Marsonauts have brought back live organisms from the Red Planet?

Sometime in the next twenty years or so, we will have the answers to these questions.

ten

There Is Life on Mars!
Colonizing the Red Planet

♂ **Around 1870, Jacob** Walz reportedly found a rich gold mine in the mountains not far from Phoenix, Arizona. When Walz died, knowledge of the mine's location was lost. Since then, many people have searched in vain for the Lost Dutchman Gold Mine. Although the first explorers may discover life on Mars, the search may prove to be like looking for the Lost Dutchman Gold Mine. Several expeditions could fail to find life, yet it could still be there—if only we looked in the right place.

On Earth, life does not only exist atop the planet. Bacteria have been found as high as 25½ miles above Earth. Organisms also live deep beneath us. In 1996, scientists concluded that an organism discovered by Carl Woese of the University of Illinois is a previously unknown type of life. Called *archaea* (meaning "ancient" in Greek), these microbes live inside volcanoes, near boiling vents at ocean bottoms, and as deep as several miles underground. Possibly our planet's oldest known form of life, archaea do not need sunlight or oxygen, but live on chemicals that rise up from deep inside Earth. The existence of archaea—called by scientists "closer to an alien species" than any other form of life on Earth—increases the likelihood that primitive organisms also live inside Mars.

Obviously we can't explore all of Mars to a depth of several miles, but it is equally certain that one or two unsuccessful searches won't convince us to give up. The search for life on Mars will continue until we have extensively explored the planet's polar caps, volcanoes, canyons, dry river and lake beds, deep underground regions, and subsurface water. While we're at it, we'll undoubtedly investigate the Mars Face and the so-called pyramids to prove that they are natural features. [Figure 10]

Planetary scientist Dr. Susan Sakimoto looks ahead at the possibilities: "If we cannot find life on Mars after a long effort, it will suggest that life is hard to start, and that at least our local neighborhood is a lonely place. But if we do find life on Mars, it will suggest that life might be easier to get going than we thought. I would be thrilled to discover that the spark of life has been lit on at least one other world. It makes the exploration of the rest of the Solar System and other systems so much more interesting!"

Although the chances that intelligent beings once inhabited Mars are slim, Martians will come into existence around the twenty-first or twenty-second century. They will think, look, and talk like Earthlings, for they will *be* human beings. One day people will settle on Mars for the same reasons people have colonized any new place.

Some Earthlings will go to Mars seeking riches. The Red Planet has plenty of iron, copper, aluminum, and deuterium (which is used in the nuclear power industry). It may have mineable deposits of silver, gold, and other valuable minerals. As Earth's supply of certain natural resources dwindles, Mars could become a source of fresh materials.

Throughout the world, there are people who suffer from hunger and violence or who feel threatened by nuclear war or pollution. Much as the Pilgrims viewed America as a safe haven, many Earthlings will welcome the chance to begin life anew on an entirely different planet.

A sense of adventure or curiosity has prompted many people on Earth to settle new places. The time is coming when people with the "pioneer spirit" will have a whole new planet to settle. As Dr. Gerald Soffen says: "I have no doubt that we humans will inhabit Mars, because it's in our genes to want to experience new things and explore new places."

Scientists may be the most eager Martian settlers. Volcanologists (experts on volcanoes) will move to Mars to study the Solar System's largest known volcanoes. Geographers (scientists who map Earth's features) and geologists (scientists who study the Earth to learn about its past) will have another world to survey. *Geo* means "Earth" in Greek, so on Mars they won't be called *geographers* and *geologists*. They may be called *areographers* and *areologists,* from Ares, the ancient Greek name for Mars.

Climatologists will move to Mars to study its climate, and hydrologists (experts on water) will arrive to hunt for water. Moreover, the search for life will be more efficient if biologists (scientists who study living organisms) and paleontologists (experts on fossils) settle on Mars instead of commuting back and forth from Earth to work there.

It may seem that, except for the search for life, the work of all these *-ologists* will be of little concern to most people. Actually, research into the Red Planet's past could contribute to the very survival of us Earthlings.

Mars demonstrates that a planet can change dramatically over time. Once warm and wet, Mars today is cold and dry. What changed Mars? Could Earth experience a major climate change that would make it impossible for us to continue living here?

Currently we are concerned that a *greenhouse effect* caused by air pollution will lead to disastrous global warming of Earth. Greenhouses, in which plants are grown year-round, are warm because their glass or plastic roofs and sides let heat in but prevent most of it from escaping. Similarly, an atmospheric blanket of carbon dioxide and other gases can trap heat, warming a planet. When we burn oil, automobile gasoline, coal, and natural gas, we release carbon dioxide (CO_2) gas into our atmosphere. Heat that would otherwise escape into space is blocked by this blanket of CO_2 and bounces back toward our planet, warming it. Other pollutants that we release intensify global warming.

The short-term effects of global warming can be pleasant. Winters are milder, heating bills are lower, and people can spend more time outdoors. Over the years, though, global warming could turn some regions into deserts while causing massive flooding in Earth's most populous areas. A big question is: How extreme must air pollution be before it causes catastrophic global warming? While admitting that air pollution is a problem, some scientists argue that it isn't a grave threat. Others say that if we don't clean up our air, disastrous climate changes are coming sooner than we think.

That's where Mars comes in. Climatologists on Mars will try to determine not only what altered its climate, but also the intensity of the processes that triggered the change. If we discover that only slight changes in conditions transformed Mars from wet and warm to cold and dry, then our Earth could be in deep trouble.

"Planets' climates are fragile," says Dr. Sakimoto. "The question is, *how* fragile?" The answer may be found on Mars.

We can look ahead and imagine how Mars might be colonized.

Each expedition that visits Mars early in the twenty-first century may leave behind the habitat in which it lived. By 2040 or 2050, there could be a dozen or more habitats scattered across Mars, each with an oxygen-making device also left in place. These habitats can serve as temporary housing for the colonists who could begin arriving around the middle of the twenty-first century.

The first Mars colony might have about 100 people, requiring three or four spacecraft to transport them. By then, we may have developed much faster spacecraft than those of today. The voyage that took the first Marsonauts six months may be reduced to only six weeks.

When the first colonists land on Mars, someone with a historic sense may step on a boulder that will become known as "Mars Rock," reminiscent of the Pilgrims' Plymouth Rock in Massachusetts. While living temporarily in their spacecraft and in the habitats left by earlier explorers, the colonists build their town, which they name Lowellville, for the man who inspired so much interest in the planet. Supply ships that have been sent ahead provide the colonists with certain essential materials and additional oxygen-making devices, but, soon after arriving on Mars, the settlement's miners and manufacturers begin producing metals, glass, cement, and plastic from native Martian materials. The first homes, houses of worship, town hall, school, and hospital may be constructed with bricks made from Mars dust. Later, large plastic domes may be set up to serve as dwellings and public buildings.

Domes will make fine greenhouses on Mars. Their clear plastic roofs and sides let in sunlight, essential for crop growth. The colonists grow corn, wheat, rice, mushrooms, and assorted fruits and vegetables. Besides providing food, the crops create more air, because plants produce oxygen. Meat is in short supply, but the colonists raise fish in indoor tanks.

The colony has been located where water was previously found, but hydrologists and miners go out to drill for more. When they hit an underground pool of water, it shoots up like an oil gusher, but the water freezes before falling back to the surface because of Mars's cold temperatures. The ice is melted and used by people and crops. Lowellville residents generate their electricity by harnessing sunlight, wind, and heat from inside Mars. Although space suits aren't needed indoors, the colonists must put them on each time they go outside. [Figure 11]

At first, the colonists consider themselves Earthlings who have been transplanted to Mars. They call Earth the "Mother Planet," much as the American colonists called England the "Mother Country." The Mars pioneers watch TV shows beamed from Earth and eagerly await the newspapers and magazines from home that arrive with each new batch of colonists. Even their first laws and officials have been decided by authorities on Earth.

But as time passes, the colonists begin to think of Mars as home. A newspaper, the *Lowellville Gazette,* is begun, followed by the rival *Mars Times.* Each year, a few families move out of the original settlement and start new towns. Within ten years of the founding of Lowellville, Mars has a dozen towns. People want to know what is happening around the planet, so TV station WMAR is established. By this time, the colonists have their own holidays. Arrival Day, the anniversary of the landing of the first colonists, is celebrated with parades and fireworks at Mars Rock. The colonists have also begun printing their own money and have adopted a red and green Martian flag. The red stands for the color of Mars as they found it, and the green for the color they expect it to become.

Sports are immensely popular on Mars. Because Mars's gravitation is only three-eighths that of Earth, people can accomplish feats that they could only dream about on the Mother Planet. Golfers drive the ball more than a quarter of a mile on Mars. Basketball is a rage, but the baskets must be raised, since every player can jump higher than Michael Jordan does on Earth. At school track meets, high jumps of about 10 feet and long jumps of 50 feet are common. A sprinter who can run 15 miles an hour on Earth can run 40 miles per hour on Mars. A baseball stadium called the Marsdome has been proposed, but the colonists are reluctant to spend a fortune on a giant dome with a home-run fence a thousand feet from home plate. [Figure 17]

Soon after reaching Mars, the colonists elect their own officials. The settlers seem to argue politics constantly. Nearly everyone complains about high taxes, because oxygen and water production are so costly. Towns quarrel over water. Saganville, for example, sits near a huge aquifer and charges high fees to pump water through pipes to Lowellville. This angers Lowellvillians, who insist that water should be shared. Saganville residents resent Lowellville because *it* expects to be named both the capital of Mars and the site of the University of Mars.

The most heated arguments involve issues affecting the entire planet. Across Mars, activists claim that nuclear power and widespread mining are threatening the environment. They hold marches and display M.A.R.S.S. (Martians Against Ruining the Solar System) bumper stickers on their Mars Rovers. Independence is another huge issue. Some people think that Earth should continue to exercise certain controls over Mars. Others argue for Martian liberty. In addition, many colonists are disgusted that the Martian Park Service, based on Earth, has designated vast sections of the Red Planet off-limits to mining and settlement. Known as the Martian National Parks, these areas are preserved for their scenic beauty or because scientists want to dig there for fossils or study the Martian climate.

Although many Martians realize that fossil hunting and climate research were prime reasons for going to Mars in the first place, there is a movement to build condominiums and golf courses on the land. Yes, there is life on Mars, declare those who want to open the whole planet to development. There is intelligent life—the colonists who within a few years have turned the Red Planet into a new home for humanity.

With its present conditions, Mars could not support a large population. The cost and difficulty of constantly having to produce more water and oxygen would limit growth. Furthermore, despite Earth's pollution, wars, and other problems, most of us would prefer a place where we can walk along a beach or hike in a forest over a planet where we need space suits just to go outside.

We may be able to change Mars's climate and atmosphere to make the planet more attractive. This is called *terraforming* (meaning changing a planet to make it resemble Earth), a word not found in many dictionaries because it won't be done for perhaps a century or more. In the case of Mars, we will want to make it warmer and wetter and have more oxygen.

At first thought, changing an entire planet seems impossible. Yet we are doing it on Earth—in a harmful way. By polluting our air, we have caused global warming. On Mars, we would change the planet to make it more conducive to life as we know it.

Terraforming raises ethical questions (issues of right and wrong). How dare we alter the environment of another planet before we show that we can care for our own? Such questions will be hashed out among authorities on Earth, the Martian government, and citizens' groups like M.A.R.S.S. For now, let's put aside the ethical issues and consider how terraforming might be accomplished.

By polluting Earth's atmosphere with carbon dioxide, we have created a harmful greenhouse effect resulting in global warming. If we could release large amounts of carbon dioxide into Mars's atmosphere, we could create a global warming that would make the planet hospitable to life.

Large amounts of carbon dioxide are frozen in Mars's polar caps, especially its South Pole. We might launch a giant orbiting mirror above Mars that will reflect sunlight toward the pole, heating it slightly and releasing the gas. Another method would be to collect material from Mars's moon Phobos, which is very dark, and spread it over Mars's South Pole. Dark materials hold heat better than light materials and would help thaw out the polar carbon dioxide. [Figure 12]

The CO_2 released from the South Pole would rise into the atmosphere, causing a greenhouse effect that would warm Mars gradually. Eventually, in places, Mars's temperature would top 32 degrees Fahrenheit, the point at which ice thaws into water.

The higher temperatures would melt underground ice, causing

rivers to flow across Mars once more. Pipelines or canals would be built to carry the river water to settlements in dry areas. At last Percival Lowell's theory of the Martian canals would have come true—centuries after he proposed the idea!

Terraforming Mars would also require the creation of a much larger oxygen supply. When it was young, our Earth didn't have enough atmospheric oxygen to support advanced forms of life. More than three billion years ago, simple organisms called algae appeared on Earth. They took in carbon dioxide and produced oxygen, eventually creating enough to support human beings and other higher kinds of life.

We could grow genetically engineered plants designed to thrive, reproduce, and generate large amounts of oxygen. Planted in various places around Mars, they would produce more and more oxygen. Within perhaps 500 years, Mars could have enough oxygen for people and animals to live there without wearing space suits. With flowing water, warmer temperatures, and plenty of oxygen, Mars could become home to many millions of people. [Figure 13]

Imagine what Mars might be like around A.D. 2500. By then, scientists know whether the Red Planet, prior to the arrival of people, had ever been home to microbes, plants, and animals. Also by then, Mars has been terraformed into a green and blue globe, with forests, flowers, and wildlife. People walk outdoors on Mars without space suits, just as they do on Earth. Only in history books are there pictures of the early colonists wearing protective clothing to survive on the surface of Mars.

Or perhaps by then, Earth will be so polluted that people will need to wear space suits to walk around on the Mother Planet, and scientists will insist that, with a lot of hard work, Earth could be made into as pleasant a world as Mars.

afterword

Mars Is Just the Beginning

♂ **When people land** on Mars, an old dream will be fulfilled and a great quest will be begun: the exploration of the Universe in search of life.

Recently we have learned that life might exist on several of the Solar System's moons. The *Galileo* probe that reached Jupiter in 1995 made exciting discoveries about Europa, one of the Giant Planet's sixteen known moons. Europa seems to have icebergs upon its cracked surface. Beneath its icy outer coat, Europa may have oceans where some type of sea life could flourish. By about 2004, NASA expects to launch a craft that will orbit Europa and reveal more about it. Eventually a *hydrobot* (water robot) may be sent to Europa. It will burrow through its icy surface and release a small submarine that will explore Europa's subsurface oceans (assuming they exist). One day astronauts may travel to this fascinating moon, then dive in a submarine beneath its surface to hunt for life.

Titan, the biggest of Saturn's more than twenty moons, might also harbor primitive organisms. After a seven-year journey, the *Cassini* craft is scheduled to arrive in orbit around Saturn in 2004. *Cassini* is supposed to release a probe that will parachute down to Titan and send back data about conditions there. As with Mars and Europa, though, human explorers may be required to search for life on Saturn's largest moon.

Perhaps we will find microbes on Mars or on another body in the Solar System. Conceivably, we will uncover fossils. Important though these discoveries would be, we would still want to find intelligent beings with whom we can communicate. Earth is probably the only place in the Solar System where such beings ever existed, but the Solar System is hardly the only place to look. Our Sun and its nine known planets and their moons are just one corner of an incredibly vast Universe.

The Universe is composed of *galaxies*—huge islands of stars traveling together through space. We reside in the Milky Way galaxy, so called because a star-rich portion of it resembles milk spilled across the sky. According to a recent estimate, the Milky Way galaxy contains a trillion (1,000,000,000,000) stars. Counting the stars in the Milky Way galaxy at the rate of three per second, it would take 10,000 years to count them all.

Just as our Sun is one star in the Milky Way, the Milky Way is one among a gigantic number of galaxies. In 1996, astronomers announced that the Hubble Space Telescope had revealed that the Universe contains more than fifty billion galaxies. The Milky Way is a rather typical galaxy. Figuring roughly a trillion stars per galaxy, the total number of stars in the Universe is fifty sextillion (50,000,000,000,000,000,000,000), give or take a zero or two. A computer counting at a rate of a billion per second would need more than a million years to count all of the stars in the Cosmos. [Figure 14]

Stars are much too hot to support life, but planets that have the proper conditions can be ideal. Until recently, astronomers did not know if any stars except the Sun had planets. Then, in the early 1990s, they began detecting planets around distant stars. They could not see these planets, but they knew they existed because their gravitation pulled their stars slightly out of their expected position. By 1998, astronomers had discovered about twelve planets orbiting stars similar to our Sun. They now figure that about one-fifth of all stars, or 10 sextillion stars, have planetary systems. Even if just one planet in a billion resembles Earth, the Universe would have 10 trillion (10,000,000,000,000) Earthlike planets that might be home to intelligent life.

NASA plans to build a telescope that may enable us to *see* Earthlike planets around faraway stars. Called the Planet Finder, the telescope's tremendous power will result largely from its location. Telescopes on Earth must gaze through Earth's air, which weakens and distorts images. The secret of the Hubble Space Telescope's great power is that it is located nearly 400 miles above Earth, beyond city lights, pollution, and most of our atmosphere. Yet even there, the instrument is hampered by space dust found in our part of the Solar System. The Planet Finder is expected to be launched into an orbit about 500 million miles from the Sun (approximately the distance of Jupiter), far beyond the obscuring dust of the inner Solar System. From there, it may be powerful enough to detect oceans and continents on Earthlike planets and to determine if their atmospheres could support life. Construction of the Planet Finder is likely to be under way, or even completed, by 2015—around the time of the first human expedition to Mars. [Figure 15]

Imagine the excitement if the Planet Finder discovers a globe with oceans, continents, and an Earthlike atmosphere orbiting a distant star. Everyone will want us to go there to see if it has intelligent life. But because of the enormous distances between stars, that is easier said than done.

So immense are interstellar distances that it is awkward to present them in miles. Proxima Centauri, the star nearest the Sun, is 25 trillion (25,000,000,000,000) miles away, or 250,000 times as far from us as is Mars. Astronomers express star distances using a unit called the *light-year,* which is the distance that light, moving at 186,282 miles a second, travels in a year. A light-year equals 5.88 trillion (5,880,000,000,000) miles. Astronomers say that Proxima Centauri is 4.3 light-years away, which also means that its light takes 4.3 years to reach us. And remember, Proxima Centauri is the *closest* star to the Sun. Other stars are hundreds, thousands, or millions of times farther away.

Today's spaceships would take incredibly long periods of time to travel to other solar systems. Say that in the year 2020 the Planet Finder locates an Earthlike planet 50 light-years away. At a speed of 25,000 miles per hour—the fastest that people have traveled in space as of 1999—it would take 1,300,000 years to travel 50 light-years to the Earthlike planet.

There are ways to overcome this problem.

We can try to communicate with extraterrestrials by radio instead of flying off in spaceships to meet them. FM (frequency modulation) radio signals travel endlessly through space at the speed of light, as do TV signals (which use FM waves). An FM radio or TV program being broadcast this moment will travel 10 light-years into space in 10 years, 25 light-years in 25 years, and so on. If beings on a distant planet aimed an instrument called a radio telescope at Earth, they might intercept our FM radio and TV shows. Perhaps at this moment, creatures on a far-off planet are listening to the 1959 World Series, an old Elvis Presley record, or a Bugs Bunny cartoon.

Since 1960, astronomers on Earth have used radio telescopes to listen for possible broadcasts from extra-solar planets (planets orbiting stars beyond the Sun). These projects are known as SETI, which refers to the Search for Extraterrestrial Intelligence, generally by means of radio telescopes.

So far, no SETI project has found an alien broadcast, but that doesn't mean there aren't any. It could be another case of the Lost Dutchman Gold Mine—not looking in the right place. There are millions of points in the sky where we might aim our radio telescopes to search for alien signals, which is why SETI researchers compare their work to looking for a needle in a cosmic haystack. But if the Planet

The world's largest radio-radar telescope, a thousand-foot-diameter dish in Arecibo, Puerto Rico. This giant instrument has been used for SETI research.

Finder locates a few Earthlike worlds, we will have some likely targets for our SETI projects.

And what if we intercepted an alien signal?

Then we could make a long space voyage knowing that somebody might be home when we arrived. Still, taking more than a million years to travel 50 light-years seems out of the question.

One solution is to build faster spaceships. If we could travel 25,000 miles per second instead of per hour, we could cut the trip length to 400 years. Currently we are too busy trying to reach Mars to devote much effort to building starships. Nonetheless, rocket scientists have plans on their drawing boards for some incredibly fast spacecraft, such as the fusion rocket, the interstellar ramjet, the ram-augmented interstellar rocket, the ion-propulsion spaceship, the antimatter starship, and the laser-powered interstellar spaceship. Perhaps one or more of these proposed craft could travel 25,000 miles per second.

We would still have a problem, however. An expedition requiring 400 years to reach a planet 50 light-years away and 400 years to return to Earth is still too long for a human lifetime. It seems that even at 25,000 miles per second—a speed so fast it would propel us from the Earth to the Moon in 10 seconds—we can't visit other solar systems. But don't give up, because there are possibilities.

The "Rip Van Winkle Plan," named for a character in an old story who falls asleep for twenty years, would place astronauts in a frozen sleep to keep them from aging during long voyages. Upon reaching their destination, they would thaw out, awaken, and conduct their exploration. They would then be refrozen for the return to Earth. If we can devise a "human antifreeze" to prevent the freezing process from destroying the body's cells, this technique might work.

Another possibility is an *interstellar space colony,* a fast-moving vehicle, several miles in diameter, that would resemble a city zooming through space. The colony will spin, creating an Earthlike gravity so that people can live on its inner surface, which would have streets, homes, businesses, schools, and parks. Plants grown in the space colony would provide food and renew the oxygen supply. Generation after generation, the travelers would live in the huge starship, always moving closer to their destination. Eventually the descendants of the original voyagers would arrive and explore the Earthlike planet. [Figure 16]

There is one more possibility. We may eventually travel even faster than 25,000 miles per second. However, according to physicist Albert Einstein's *special theory of relativity,* there is a cosmic speed limit: A spacecraft can approach but never reach the speed of light—186,282 miles per second. The bottom line seems to be that there is no way for us to travel to a planet 50 light-years away in less than 50 years. Amazingly, nature has provided a way around this obstacle.

Einstein also explained that, because time is relative to speed, it can work in surprising ways. Astronauts speeding along in a spaceship age more slowly than they would have had they remained on Earth. *Time dilation,* as this effect is called, has been proved in laboratories.

Because of time dilation, astronauts who travel at thousands of miles per hour return to Earth a fraction of a second younger than they would be had they not left home. The effect becomes more extreme at much faster speeds. Imagine twenty-five-year-old twins, one of whom is an astronaut. The astronaut blasts off on what seems to her to be a twenty-year voyage at 90 percent of the speed of light, or 168,000 miles per second. She returns to Earth forty-five years old, only to find that her twin is sixty-five years old. The astronaut does not feel that she has cheated time, for during her space flight the hours and days seemed to pass at the same rate she was accustomed to on Earth. But twenty years at her high rate of speed equaled forty years of Earth-time.

Time dilation has an even greater impact at 184,000 miles a second, or 99 percent of the speed of light. Imagine that a forty-five-year-old astronaut leaves his two-year-old grandson on Earth and embarks on what seems to him to be a twelve-year voyage at 99 percent of the speed of light. The astronaut returns to Earth fifty-seven years old. The young grandson he left on Earth is now about ninety years old—older than his grandfather.

Traveling at virtually 100 percent of the speed of light, time would slow to a crawl for the space voyager in relation to Earth-time. Theoretically, an astronaut approaching 186,282 miles per second could travel to the farthest known reaches of the Universe—billions of light-years away—within a single human lifetime.

Today the idea of building vessels that can travel near the speed of light seems far-fetched. But what if we discover life on Mars, and the Planet Finder locates a few blue and green worlds that seem to be twins of Earth? For that matter, what if we learn that Mars and all the other bodies in the Solar System are lifeless? Won't our curiosity demand that we venture farther and farther from Earth in search of life, especially intelligent life?

Someday, human beings may zip around the Universe as effortlessly as twenty-first-century astronauts will drive across Mars. When that happens, let us remember that humanity's greatest quest—the search for extraterrestrial life—began with the fascinating Red Planet, Mars.

For Further Reading

Asimov, Isaac. *The Red Planet: Mars*. Milwaukee: Gareth Stevens Publishing, 1988; revised and updated by Francis Reddy, 1994.

Barbree, Jay, and Martin Caidin, with Susan Wright. *Destination Mars: Mars in Art, Myth, and Science*. New York: Penguin Studio, 1997.

Brewer, Duncan. *Mars*. New York: Marshall Cavendish, 1992.

Clarke, Arthur C. *The Snows of Olympus: A Garden on Mars*. New York: Norton, 1995.

Cole, Michael D. *Living on Mars: Mission to the Red Planet*. Springfield, New Jersey: Enslow, 1999.

Corrick, James A. *Mars*. New York: Franklin Watts, 1991.

DeSomma, Vincent V. *The Mission to Mars and Beyond*. New York: Chelsea House, 1992.

Kelch, Joseph W. *Millions of Miles to Mars: A Journey to the Red Planet*. Parsippany, New Jersey: Julian Messner/Silver Burdett, 1995.

Landau, Elaine. *Mars*. New York: Franklin Watts, 1991.

Sheehan, William. *The Planet Mars: A History of Observation and Discovery*. Tucson: The University of Arizona Press, 1996.

Simon, Seymour. *Mars*. New York: Morrow, 1987.

Vogt, Gregory L. *Mars*. Brookfield, Connecticut: The Millbrook Press, 1994.

Wilford, John Noble. *Mars Beckons*. New York: Knopf, 1990.

Zubrin, Robert, with Richard Wagner. *The Case for Mars: The Plan to Settle the Red Planet and Why We Must*. New York: The Free Press, 1996.

SOME WEB SITES TO EXPLORE

The Mars Millennium Project **www.mars2030.net**

NASA Homepage **www.nasa.gov**

NASA Office of Space Science **www.spacescience.nasa.gov**

NASA Planetary Exploration **www.jpl.nasa.gov**

NASA Planetary Sciences **nssdc.gsfc.nasa.gov/planetary/planetary_home.html**

NASA Planetary Photojournal **photojournal.jpl.nasa.gov**

Credits

PHOTOS IN TEXT:

National Optical Astronomy Observatories: i

NASA and the Lunar and Planetary Institute: pages ii, iii, iv, vi, viii, 1, 4, 5, 11, 20, 29, 46, 69, 75, 77, 79, 81, 84, 86, 87, 89, 91, 92, 93, 95, 103, 112, 115, 124

Library of Congress: pages 8, 9, 12, 23, 27, 30, 64, 67

Yerkes Observatory: page 14

North Wind Picture Archives: page 17

Stock Montage, Inc., Chicago: page 24

Lowell Observatory Photographs: pages 34, 36, 43, 45

The New York Times: page 39, copyright (c) 1907 by The New York Times Co. Reprinted by permission.

U.S. Department of the Interior, National Park Service, Edison National Historic Site: page 47

Archive Photos: pages 54, 58, 60

J. Allen Hynek Center for UFO Studies: page 56

Harold Bloom: pages 39, 71

Arecibo Observatory: page 128

COLOR INSERT PHOTOS:

Stock Montage, Chicago: Figures 1, 2

National Optical Astronomy Observatories/National Science Foundation/N.A. Sharp: Figure 3

NASA and the Lunar and Planetary Institute: Figures 4, 6, 7, 8, 9, 10, 11, 14, 15, 16, 18

(c) Michael Carroll: Figures 5, 12, 13, 17

Index

Note: Page numbers for illustrations are in italics.

Index

R

Radio, 65-68, 127
Radio telescopes, 127-128, *128*
"Rip Van Winkle Plan," 128-129
Robinson, Mansfield, 68
Robotic spacecraft, 3, 104, 107
Rocks, of Mars, 3, 83, 97-98
    analyzing, 106, 112
    as meteorites on Earth, 90-96
Russia, space program of, 72-73, 76, 81, 89, 105

S

Sagan, Carl, 74-76, 76, 80, 83
Sakimoto, Susan, 107, 116, 118
Satellites, first human-made, 72
Schiaparelli, Giovanni Virginio, 1, *23*, 23-25, 32, 41
Score, Roberta, 92, 94
Searles, Father George, 42
Seasons, Mars, 17
SETI (Search for Extraterrestrial Intelligence), 99, 127-128
Shklovskii, Iosif S., 72
"Single-gas-cloud theory," 22
Slipher, Earl C., 72
SNC meteorites, from Mars on Earth, 92
Soffen, Gerald, 86-87, 89, 96, 105
    on curiosity, 108, 117
Soil, analyzing, 85-87, 105-106
Solar system
    Earth as center of, 8-10, *9*, 12-15
    origin of, 22, 93
Space probes
    to Mars, 81-85, 104-105
    to moons and planets, 73, 124-125
Space stations, 109-110, 113
Spacecraft, *See also* Space probes
    and distances between stars, 127-130
    on Mars, 81-82, 104, 111
    robotic, 3, 104, 107
Special theory of relativity, 129
Spencer, John, 97-102
Sputnik I, 72
Stansberry, John, 97-99, 102
Stars, 1, 5-6, 125-127
Sun, 13, 22
Swift, Jonathan, 20-22

T

Telescopes, 13, 15, 25, 31-32, 126
    at observatories, 33, *34*, 39-40, 69
    radio, 127-128, *128*
Television, 82-83, 110-112, 127
Terraforming, 122-123
Tesla, Nikola, 65
Thiel, Rudolf, 70
Thollon, Louis, 26
Time dilation, 129-130
Todd, David, 65-66
Tombaugh, Clyde W., 44
Topography, of Mars, 78, *84, 86*, 97-98

U

UFOs. *See* Flying saucers
United States, 84-85
    and meteorites, *91,* 92, *92*
    space program of, 2-3, 72-73, 76, 81-87, 89
Universe
    Earth as center of, 8-10, *9*
    life in, 99, 101, 124-130

V

Vaucouleurs, Gérard de, 70
Venus, 22-23, 70, 73
Viking missions, 81-87, 89
Von Mädler, Johann, 18

W

War of the Worlds, The, 2, 46-50, 54, 59, 60
Water, on Mars, 35, 78-80, 97-98, 105
    and colonization, 119, 121
    in polar caps, 87, 122-123
    previous existence of, 3, 92
    speculations of, 1, 16, 18
Wells, H. G., 2, 46-50
Whiting, Lilian, 38
Woese, Carl, 115
Wood, R. W., 62-63
Wright, Ian, 96

Y

Yerkes Observatory, 39-40

Z

Zare, Richard, 96

About the Author

Dennis Brindell Fradin grew up in Chicago, Illinois, and earned a B.A. in creative writing from Northwestern University. He was an elementary school teacher for twelve years and is the author of over one hundred nonfiction books, ranging in subject from the fifty states to medicine to astronomy. In 1989, Dennis Fradin was honored as an Outstanding Contributor to Education by the National College of Education in Evanston, Illinois.

Dennis Fradin is the author of *Hiawatha: Messenger of Peace,* which was named a Notable Children's Trade Book in the Field of Social Studies; *"We Have Conquered Pain": The Discovery of Anesthesia,* which was a Junior Library Guild selection; and *The Planet Hunters: The Search for Other Worlds,* which was named an American Library Association Best Book for Young Adults and a Nonfiction Honor Book by *Voice of Youth Advocates.*

Mr. Fradin is married to Judith Bloom Fradin, who is herself a writer and who helped obtain the pictures for *Is There Life on Mars?* The Fradins have three grown children and one grandchild and live in Evanston, Illinois.